Anna didn't care about her new home.
Nothing could ever make the place
more than a roof over her head, a
bitter mockery of the graceful farmhouse
where she had lived so happily. She
was leaving her friends and everything
she knew. She might as well be going to
Australia as to live in Cheshire, she
thought. Dan didn't understand . . .
It was never so bad for a woman, Dan
thought. She had a home to run, no
matter where she lived. He had nothing.
His hands felt unused – he longed to
milk cattle, to tend a calving cow, to
take one of his pedigree beasts to a
show . . . but it was all over. He was
no longer a farmer.
The future seemed bleak indeed . . .
until the animals began to arrive . . .

Also by Joyce Stranger

and published by Corgi Books

Joyce Stranger

Never Count Apples

CORGI BOOKS

NEVER COUNT APPLES

A CORGI BOOK 0552 10054 4

Originally published in Great Britain by
Harvill Press Ltd.

PRINTING HISTORY
Harvill Press edition published 1974
Corgi edition published 1976
Corgi edition reprinted 1976
Corgi edition reprinted 1977
Corgi edition reissued 1983
Copyright © 1974 Joyce Stranger Limited

Conditions of sale
1: This book is sold subject to the condition that it
shall not, by way of trade *or otherwise*, be lent, re-sold,
hired out or otherwise *circulated* without the publisher's
prior consent in any form of binding or cover other than
that in which it is published *and without a similar
condition including this condition being imposed on
the subsequent purchaser.*
2: This book is sold subject to the Standard Conditions
of Sale of Net Books and may not be re-sold in the U.K.
below the net price fixed by the publishers for the book.

Corgi Books are published by Transworld Publishers Ltd.,
Century House, 61–63 Uxbridge Road,
Ealing, London W.5.
Made and printed in Great Britain by
Hunt Barnard Printing Ltd., Aylesbury, Bucks.

ACKNOWLEDGEMENTS
I wish to thank everybody who has helped me with this book,
and in particular Judy Pilling, breeder of the Gorsefield
Alsatians, who has read and checked the manuscript for me.

To Belinda Pilling

One of the central incidents in this book happened to my own Alsatian and her two litter brothers. The rest of the book is fiction and neither the characters nor the places exist.

CHAPTER ONE

'It's no use brooding,' Dan said, anger roughening his voice. 'We had no choice. I tried everything.'

Anna did not even turn her head. She stared blindly out of the window. Compton Hall had been their home for eighteen years. This was the place Dan had brought her to, as a bride. Here she had lived and worked, and loved working, all those long years. Here memories had been forged, until the farm and the land were part of her, belonging to her, and she to them. Here she had thought to die, and to see her grandsons inherit and continue the long tradition that had been built over the centuries.

She could not speak.

Dan looked at his wife helplessly. She was as slender as the day he had first seen her; a tiny woman, beautifully made, her apparent delicacy belying her physique. Her elegant hands and feet were also small; her face reminded him of a drowsy kitten, the bones fine drawn under a clear tanned skin, the slanting eyes grey-green, their expression aloof and mysterious. She had intrigued him from the moment he met her, walking with her copper-coloured red setter, in the woods beyond his home.

The woods blurred the horizon now. They were January-bare and bleak beyond endurance. They would never again see them green with the breath-taking light-holding sheen of spring. They would never again see the tight buds on the azaleas that rode the bank at the end of the garden. Anna had planted ten new bushes every year. In spring they were a blaze of colour, clear and beautiful; a riot of

7

red and scarlet and cherry; of gold and amber and soft downy yellow; of white, and cream, and honey. Anna loved colour.

Dan towered above his wife, his burly body seeming too big for the clothes he wore, a massive chest straining the well-cut dark shirt, his thick neck, reddened by weather, rising from the open collar, crowned by an arrogant head, the dark curly hair worn shorter than was fashionable. His mouth was set in a hard line as he watched his wife. Anna wasn't even trying to make it easy. He felt as badly as she.

Perhaps he felt worse.

'Damn everything,' he thought bitterly. He would miss it all much more than his wife. He had been born in this house. He had played round the barns and the byres and the stables; had slept in the little attic under the eaves that had been Philip's room for the past twelve years. He had mounted his first pony in the cobbled yard which was still exactly as it had been in his grandfather's day.

He could see the pony now. Bracken, a gentle little dark creature, a cross between a Shetland and a New Forest pony, with a black mane and pretty head and wise brown eyes. He had loved Bracken passionately. The pony had been the first living creature that he, personally, had ever owned.

He had slept in that little attic room until he married, when his parents had moved to the cottage, and he had brought Anna home and taken over the master bedroom, which looked towards the woods.

He had been very proud of his home. It was an old house, half-timbered. The rooms inside were beamed with black oak that had been oiled for centuries and still shone with the glow of care. The mullioned windows were bright. Anna had been unable to leave them dirty, even though the demolishers were moving in in two days' time. When the azaleas bloomed they would not be here to see, and within a few weeks they too would be gone, dragged up by the roots to make way for the motorway that arrowed towards them through the distant fields, the bare earth an angry gash against the soft blue sky.

He had done everything he could to stop them. Or had he? A niggle of doubt worried at his mind. There must have been some way. The house was history in itself. Centuries of care could not be flung away so lightly, so casually. There had been Leighs here fighting for the King when Cromwell ran amok over England; Leighs had taken part in every major war. His great-uncle had won the Victoria Cross for gallantry. Now there would never be Leighs here again.

He looked back at the line of the new road, cutting through the grass, scything towards them, the bare red mud a raging sore, a flamboyant symbol of progress. Within weeks it would stride across the site of his home, laying waste the garden that had taken centuries to grow, destroying Anna's contribution to the place she had come to love, and nothing of it would be left. Anger choked him. His mouth was suddenly sour, and he felt sick.

It was so bloody unfair. How could the world have come to this? How could a man be thrust from his home as casually as a horse trampled an ant in the grass? Did no one care about people any more? Was it only things that mattered? Material possessions; fitted carpets and washing machines and colour television sets owned by fat men in sleek motor cars, who raced along the motorways, eating up the miles, going from nowhere to nowhere fast, their minds full of nothing but the food they were going to eat, the drinks they were going to drink, the girls they were going to make, and the deals they were going to clinch, the big deals that laid someone else low, and about which they could brag tomorrow in the City.

He had done everything he could. He had done more than was reasonable, mortgaging money he had not got to fight the planners. He had enlisted the help of the villagers, of the local Member of Parliament, who had backed his fight; had thrown away capital he needed in an attempt to keep his home.

It had been useless.

The motorway was coming, like it or not, and he was not the only one to suffer. Old Noakes had lost his little cottage, and gone to rot in a Home in the town. Noakes, who was free as a lark on the wing, and had never known the rub and irritation of living with others; who had looked after his three pigs and his dozen hens and done odd jobs round the village for nearly eighty years. No one cared about him. The old man was dying of grief, but what did that matter. Age had no place in a young and arrogant society that was daily growing more cruel.

The motorway would run across the yard where he had ridden his first pony; where he had struggled to make ends meet, with only one man to help him in the lean years after the war; where he had fought to restore the land that had gone sour with neglect while he and his father were both absent, fighting. His mother and his sisters had carried on alone, working with the old men in the village, but they had been unable to keep the farm in good heart.

He had battled through power cuts, milking the cattle by hand, lugging the huge oil heaters across the fields in the dark, bringing them out of the barn where they had lain unused for years, to save his pigs and his hens from dying of cold. He had run the tractor all night, to work the fans in the henhouse, lest the birds suffocate. He would have liked to throttle the strikers with his bare hands. He had sat with calving cows and foaling mares, thinking of the years ahead, of tradition unbroken, of Leighs still farming when Elizabeth was dead and Charles was king, and for years to follow that; of great-grandchildren he would never see repeating the age-old sanities; sitting in the quiet barn, milking a goat, listening to the animals' soft breathing; hearing the clank of churns; watching the cattle come home through the sunlit fields, full udders swinging.

He had imagined his heirs living as he lived, in the old farmhouse that was a treasure house of memories; fighting the weather, the gales that lashed the harvests, the frosts that froze the water supply, the floods that ruined the crops.

He had weathered the foot-and-mouth epidemic of 1967 and saved his pedigree beasts. He looked out now at the empty fields, where no cattle moved. There, under the poplars, had grazed his beautiful Jersey herd. He had bred them himself, had been proud of the pedigree, proud of the cups and rosettes that they won at the Dairy Shows. He could see them so clearly in his mind. Griselda and Greta; Gaygirl and Gretchen; Goldie and Goblina; Gamin and Gasetta. They had always had names that began with G for some reason that escaped him, but had been decreed by Lisetta who had been five when the first was brought to the house to replace the Friesians that had been Dan's father's joy.

She had named the cow Glory, and Glory's calf was Gina. It had been the beginning of a family tradition, a small shared family joke. Lisetta was sixteen now, as small and slender as her mother, with the same wideboned face and shining grey-green eyes. She reminded her father of his courting days, when Anna had looked as young as Lisa did now. Their daughter was as alien to him as another man's child, full of fire and anger, refusing to help about the farm or to help her mother, unable, ever, to tell them anything she did or thought or hoped.

'I hate you,' she had shouted, only last night, as the ponies went into the horse-box to begin the long journey to the new house he had bought in a village as distant as he could find. 'You could have saved us. Other people have. You didn't try.'

It wasn't fair.

It wasn't bloody well fair.

He had gone to the Bleeding Stag for the last time, and sat, morose and angry, unable to talk to the friends who sympathised in silence and had no idea what to say, drinking to drown the ache that had become permanent inside him, so that it hurt to think, or talk, or to eat, or to remember. And Anna didn't help. She behaved as if he had been responsible, as if he had not even tried to save their home.

He walked towards her, wanting to touch her hair, to hold her for comfort, to tell her he had spent as much as he dared, but she moved away from him, to look out of the other window. She had grown more and more prickly and aloof in the last few months.

Anna stared out at the garden. There were the azaleas. Beyond them were woods which, in a few weeks' time, would be starred with windflowers and primroses; as quiet and peaceful as they had been when she walked with Copper, long ago.

She was the granddaughter of a farmer, and farming was in her blood. Her mother had married a solicitor and gone gladly to live a suburban existence, away from animals. Anna hated suburbia. She detested the red brick box that her parents bought, in the stockbroker belt at the very edge of the old town, a house owing its character to fake stone and mock beams, a spuriousness that hid none of its modernity.

Anna disliked coffee mornings and tennis parties and the slick talk of intellectual books that she thought pretentious and boring. She hid her love of poetry, and escaped whenever she could to the country, taking with her her red setter, a lunatic dog that made her laugh as he chased his tail or raced after swallows, always hoping to catch one, one bright sunny day.

She walked along the woodland ride to look at the horses in the big field, to pet them and talk with them. Her father would not let her ride. His brother

12

had been killed in a jumping accident and he hated horses. Anna loved them with a passionate love. She bought horse books and pony books, and when she was small pretended she had her own pony. He was creamy white and she named him Silver. He had a scarlet saddle, and she rode him with a silver whip in her hand, winning at all the pony club shows, jumping fearlessly over high fences, training him until he could leap like a cat, and turn on a sixpence, and fly with her over the Common. He was so real to her that even now, thinking back, she could visualise every hair, the way his mane had flowed, his elegant tail and neat little dark hooves. Her father, a sentimental man, named her Dolly Daydream, because she spent so much time thinking about her imaginary horse that the world around her was often unreal.

There had been a pony like him in the big field near her home; a silver grey that she loved to watch as he rolled in the sun, his legs kicking merrily, or when he trotted with the other horses, the wind streaming mane and tail. She spent endless hours there, thinking of nothing in particular, wishing the horses were hers, and there she met Dan.

The horses belonged to his father. He came one afternoon to fetch his gelding, and saw her standing there, longing in her face. The wind blew her hair about her cheeks; the grey-green cat eyes were remote, as if she did not belong to the world about her, or acknowledge its reality.

Dan admired Copper, and Anna came suddenly to life, and asked about the horses, and went into the field to stroke them, feeling as if she had been given the key to Heaven. Soon, she spent all her spare time at the farm, and was accepted as one of the family. Dan's parents liked her, and her parents accepted Dan. The Leighs were an important family. They had been part of the old village for centuries

13

and were good and careful farmers. The land was rich.

Dan was ten years older than Anna. He valued his wife, and watched her grow to love the house and cherish it as Leigh wives had always cherished it. They needed nothing. The furniture, matched to the house, was old and treasured. Only the big soft chairs and settee were almost new, but even they were covered with chintzes that echoed the curtains and blended with the rooms and were completely right for the house.

Anna was picturing the rooms as she had known them, and it was small comfort to come back to emptiness; to marks on the wallpaper where the dressingtable and chests had stood, to the bare dark boards where footsteps echoed, to the curtainless windows that looked out over the silent fields.

Only a month ago she had fed the calves with buckets of milk, standing in the big byre, watching them suck greedily, laughing at them. She loved the small animals most of all. Now they were sold too. The lump in her throat was too big to swallow; it was choking her. She dared not speak, lest tears flood down her face and become uncontrollable. Everything she loved was being destroyed. At that moment she hated Dan with all her heart, for giving her so much and then letting it be taken away from her.

She would not look at the azaleas. She shut her eyes but that only brought memories of the haze of white on the hawthorn hedge and the daffodils that would soon have glowed in every corner of the garden, and the bed of massed crocus which, every year, she threaded with a maze of cotton, to protect the succulent flowers from the birds. She looked, instead, at the fields.

There was a cock pheasant in the corner, down by the ditch. He walked slowly, regally, his brilliant head and neck shining in the sun, his chestnut feathers glittering, his long tail flicking up and down as he moved. Somehow, he made the place look much emptier.

'For God's sake, let's go,' Dan said gruffly.

Anna turned away and walked blindly out of the room, and down the wide oak staircase into the sunlit hall. Sunbeams gilded the floor, streamed through the mullioned windows, lit the bare walls, shone on bleak emptiness. Little ghosts sighed in the corners and played through the sunbeams; ghosts of Lisetta, crawling down the passage after one of the cats, and of Philip, playing with the dogs, teasing them at Christmas with balloons that they batted gaily until they broke and left the animals searching for something that had vanished like a bubble, mystifying them completely, while Philip laughed.

There were other ghosts too, of children long ago, of Dan himself in his schooldays, and of his father before them. And as the front door slammed irrevocably shut behind them, there were ghosts in the yard. Ghosts of the lowing cattle and the racing hens; of the little black pig that she had reared, coming into the kitchen for its bottle; of the brown lamb that had waited for titbits, bleating noisily; of the dogs they had owned, and of the ponies, and of her beautiful brood mare, Syrena, who had died the year before.

There was nothing left to say. There was nothing left to do. They would come back, perhaps, in after years, but the house would be gone, and everything would have changed. The busy highway would swathe the grassy fields, would drive through the growing woods, would obliterate everything they had known. It would save a million men a million minutes a year, would cater for the dinosaurian double lorries that thundered across the continent, would commemorate the Age of the Motor Car; the Age of Progress; the Age of Industry; the completion of the changes started by the Industrial Revolution.

15

Could he have done more? Dan wondered as Anna climbed into the car, and sat staring in front of her, fighting to keep her serenity. He could not challenge bureaucracy alone. He had wanted to hit with his fists, to find faces to batter, faces for the featureless men in Whitehall who decreed his farm should die. Had they ever axed their own homes or turned themselves out into the streets, he wanted to ask. He wanted to shout in the Press, to stir up the village, to make the intangible real so that he could defeat and defy it. But there was no one man responsible; no one man to hate or blame. There was only a system that had grown over the years and that everyone accepted.

Those he sought to fight were as tenuous as the balloons that the dogs played with and burst and hunted endlessly. He rammed the car into gear.

Anna cried out.

From the open doorway of the barn came the grey cat that had been missing for three weeks, and behind her stalked six tiny kittens. She looked up at the car and wailed.

Damn, thought Dan. Damn and damn and damn again.

He switched off the engine. The cat couldn't be left behind. So that was what she had been up to, silly little thing. If they had known before they could have taken care of her and found the kittens homes. Now they would start in a strange place with a cat they hadn't intended to take; a cat they thought must have died, as she had been missing so long.

Anna took the food out of the picnic hamper and put the cat and her family inside. She could still say nothing. The ache in her throat was unbearable. The house and the woods had never looked so beautiful. If only it had rained, and they had left on a grey day with the sky echoing her sorrow.

She put the hamper on the back seat of the car. Dan started the engine again, and shot out through

16

the gate and down the lane, anxious to leave the place, to put it all behind him, to begin life anew.

In spite of herself, Anna looked back. The black and white house stood bravely under the trees, and there was a blackbird singing on the thorn beside the gate. His small voice echoed, even above the engine note of the car. The sun shone from a cloudless sky, brightening the green, glittering on the hawthorn and last year's traveller's joy that clung to all the hedges, hinting at the ghosts of the past; the golden brown cattle that browsed in the fields and the horses that had hung their heads over the white barred gate.

Within weeks it would all be gone and they would be forgotten. The site on which their home had stood for centuries would lie under concrete and macadam.

Anna could see nothing for tears. She knew how Eve felt when she was driven from Paradise. But the scientists had done away with God and she had no hope left.

CHAPTER TWO

There was nothing to say as they drove down the long miles that spanned the distance between their old home and the new. Anna looked bleakly at the scenery, but saw nothing either. She only saw the azalea bank as it had been for two perfect seasons; she had completed the planting three autumns ago. It had been a symbol of her love for the place. Each Leigh wife had left her mark behind her; one had made the water garden where the tiny stream had been landscaped to tumble in miniature waterfalls over rocks that were weathered with years, and blended into the ground.

Beyond that another Leigh wife had planted a

garden of roses; big rose bushes that spilled gleaming petals on the grass; moss roses that scented the evening air; tiny golden roses, fragile as mothwings, their delicate elongated buds, tinged with deep yellow, opening into pale creamy masses, smothering the branches. They bloomed the summer long, and Anna could see them from her kitchen as she worked.

Her mother-in-law had planted a heather garden; leaves deep green and olive; golden green and silver green; and flowers as varied; masses of white tipped with yellow; masses of purple, the colour of a dark grape; masses of lilac, and masses of mauve-red, ranged in a long bed that caught the morning sun. The sudden sprays of white were the first blooms of spring, and after them came snowdrops, and multi-coloured crocuses; narcissi and daffodils, and the brilliant vivid slash of tulips. The garden had taken years to build, and had been one of her major joys.

It wasn't fair. It wasn't fair. It wasn't fair.

Anna clenched her fists. She knew she was being childish. Life never was fair, and who was she that she should be immune? Yet all the same the thought beat bitterly in her mind. She tried to thrust it away, looking at a Norman church set under a tree-clad hill, the weather vane on its castellated top an odd little shape that she suddenly realised was intended to be a pouncing cat. At the other end of the vane was a mouse.

The church vanished, replaced by a street of old cottages, sunk into a cliff, their backs against the hill. She wondered at the builder who had made them, striking into the rock. The rooms at the back could be little more than caves. How could anyone live in perpetual dark, lighted only by lamplight? She thought of her long low room and the evening light spilling through the curtains on to the polished floor, of the shaggy rug on which the old dog lay at night. Meg had died three months before they had to move and they had not replaced her. No more animals. Since they had lost everything they had loved, they would take nothing with them but the two horses. That at least they had promised to Lisetta and Phil.

The two children were staying at the vicarage until the end of the school year. Lisetta was sitting her O-level examinations, and Phil had not wanted to come with them, alone. It would be bad enough without his friends. If he missed his sister too, it would be hell, he said passionately. Yet he and Lisa quarrelled like monkeys when they were together.

The village ended and they were among fields again; fields where other men's cattle grazed peacefully, at ease. Fields in which there were farmhouses, and men who were busy in byre and barn and stable; men whose homes still belonged to them, and who worked in happy unawareness of others thrust out by unfeeling bureaucrats. The tangled last year's seedlings on the hedge were a sudden swirling mist. Anna blinked, and swallowed.

Dan drove on, concentrating grimly on the road ahead, watching the signposts that signalled the way. He had taken the long road, avoiding the motorway, hating every mile of it and all that it stood for. He had lain awake the night before, wishing passionately that he had been born into a kinder age, an age where experience and expertise counted and older men had their place. Now, he felt old and useless, forcibly retired long before his time. Who would employ a man who had been a farmer all his life? What did he know, apart from the way to rear pigs and sheep and cattle, and the prices of crops? Where could he go to find work?

The feeling of futility was creeping back. It had first overwhelmed him when he began to look for a place to live. Land prices and house prices were astronomical. His own home was at the edge of the Cotswolds, where the fold and lie of the hills under their cloak of trees had always gladdened his eyes. He could find nothing near.

He could not afford to go South. He had a huge overdraft and no bank would lend him more to start in another place. He needed money to live; and the compensation for his own home took no account of the years that had gone into making the land, into putting it in good heart, into breeding the herd, and he had little choice when he came to make the final decision.

He had come at last to Cheshire where land was cheaper. Even then, he was shocked at the price he had to pay for two old cottages and two acres of ground. He needed room for the horses. And there was a field he could rent beside his land.

The paddock was sour ground, untilled for years. Vandals had smashed the windows of both cottages, had stripped the paper from the walls, had ripped and torn the guttering. The landlord was glad to sell. The property stood at the end of a long lane and he had no other offers, though that was a fact that he did not reveal.

The end of the lane led through a footpath to the school which both Lisetta and Philip could attend. Beyond the paddock was a little river, where Dan saw an otter slide down the bank and dive into the water, and across the river were woodlands. There were no plans to build, both landlord and agent said.

Dan intended to knock the two cottages into one; to turn the two high-ceilinged and ill-proportioned downstairs rooms into a long room spanning the width of the property, with new windows overlooking the woods. He would lower the ceilings, giving the room better balance, and tear out the ugly Victorian cupboards and put in modern shelving and better lighting. Painted white and properly furnished, it would make a beautiful living-room.

Anna could not see the possibilities when they first visited the cottages. She only saw the ugliness;

the filthy floors, the stones that the lads had flung through the windows, the broken glass that lay everywhere, the minute dark kitchens, and the unexpectedly and absurdly vast bathrooms, both big enough to house an old-fashioned three-piece suite, and total wasted space. The landing was so tiny that she and Dan could not even pass one another there, and the stairs were steep and narrow, rising from a cramped hall. The front door was hideous, filled with Victorian glass that appeared to have defeated even the vandals.

Outside was worse. The corrugated iron porch was ramshackle, the gutters were torn away from the roof and tiles had been stolen. There was an old shed, through which daylight shone on piles of sacking and a rusty lawn-roller. The path was breakneck, unevenly cobbled, and puddled from recent rain. Dampness brooded on the air. The overcast sky echoed Anna's desolation. She would never settle here.

That had been six months before. Builders had been busy and the house had been renovated. Dan had been back, and approved the work, but Anna had not cared to go again. Nothing could ever make the place anything better than a roof over her head, a bitter mockery of the graceful farmhouse where she had lived so long. She was leaving her friends and everything she knew. She felt as if she were emigrating. She might as well be going to Australia as to live in Cheshire, she thought, and longed for the clock to go back, for the days to slip into reverse, and bring her to sanctuary again. If only she had died when Philip was born, as she nearly did. She would have been spared this agony. Dan didn't understand. Dan would never understand.

If only he could go back, Dan thought, as he turned along a winding lane and drove past a castle that stood arrogantly on a little hill, its moat reddened by the evening sun. Anna would never realise how he felt. It was never so bad for a woman. She had a home to run, no matter where she lived. He had nothing. His hands felt unused, without the cattle to milk and the farmyard chores waiting for him. He longed to ted hay under a calving cow; to deliver a calf and watch it suck, its small tail wagging; to take one of his pedigree beasts to the next Show and gloat over the red rosette attached to its stall; to listen to the admiring comments made by other men who did not know the cow was his.

That was over. He was no longer a farmer. He was part of the world of men who cared nothing about beasts, and he was lost. He pulled into a layby, and Anna gave him sandwiches and coffee, and said nothing at all. Behind them, the cat wailed suddenly.

'We've no food for her,' Anna said.

'There's milk,' said Dan.

He drank his coffee scalding hot and burnt his mouth, but the need to feed a hungry creature was paramount. He poured milk into the cup and Anna took the basket and set it on her knee. The cat looked up at them when they opened it, trusting them completely, glad to be reunited with them, even though she herself had chosen to hide with her litter until they were old enough to run.

She was a smoky-grey cat with short plush fur and bright green eyes that were now narrowed as she smelled milk. She drank daintily and hungrily. Anna lifted one of the kittens and held it against her face. It was small and its purr was a heartfelt throb of contentment. It was a reminder of all she had lost, of the many other tiny creatures she had reared, and the ache in her throat was too hard to control and the tears came, regardless, so that she turned her head away from Dan and stared out at the woods beyond the layby, and held the kitten until it squealed for mercy and Smoke reached up and tapped her hand angrily.

Anna put the kitten back in the basket and Dan handed her his handkerchief.

He drove out on to the road again. There were miles to go before they slept.

The sun died in a streak of scarlet. Lamplight softened the streets and patched the hills and spoke of comfort, and Dan turned the radio on, to try to change the atmosphere, which was thick with sorrow.

A woman's voice was singing.

> Home no more home to me,
> Whither shall I wander . . .

'Oh, Christ,' Dan said, and switched it off again.

Silence lay heavy about them, broken only by the whisper of the wheels on the road and the busy whirr of the windscreen wipers cleaning away the newly falling rain that echoed Anna's tears.

CHAPTER THREE

The cottages had been transformed since Anna had last seen them. The downstairs rooms had been blended into one large room, its french windows opening on to a garden that was a wasteland of grass and a morass from the recent rain. Beyond the hedge was a vista of trees, not yet in leaf. The two kitchens had been made into one and had been modernised. The resulting room was still quite small and painted white. It was well equipped, and totally strange, a sterile characterless place, as unlike as it could be from the big warm kitchen that she had left at Compton Hall, where a vast hearth occupied the inglenook and men and animals sprawled content. There was nowhere for Smoke here, or the kittens.

Only the two heads peering hopefully over the fence were familiar. The garden, at that point, bordered the field where the horses were to live. Tarquin and Sonny Boy had already arrived. Tarquin was waiting, his big patient eyes gazing interestedly at the lights in the cottage. It was not yet dark, but it was too dark to see to cook, and Anna wanted to make up a packet of soup that would add a hot dish to the cold meat and salad that she had brought with her.

Dan went out to the horses. He felt lost. Beyond him, in the farther field, another man's cattle cropped the grass, and it seemed impossible that for the first time in all his life there should be no cow of his to cure of some minor ill, to watch over while she calved, to consider at milking time. No Show to plan for. No aim to living.

Tarquin came at his call and rubbed against his master's shoulder, avid for attention. He was a big solemn horse, as safe as an arm-chair to ride, and Lisetta was always begging for a more spirited animal. She loved Tarquin, but he never challenged her skill. He plodded quietly on his own way, watching a world that was endlessly absorbing, and had been for all of his fifteen years of life.

Sonny Boy was very different. He was a small brown pony, with unhappy eyes, and not used to any of them. They had only owned him for a month before they moved. Philip's pony, Beau, who had been part of the family for twenty-five years, had developed cancer, and Dan had had to shoot him. Philip would not wait until they moved. He must have a new pony, now.

Sonny Boy had been for sale, and Dan had bought him, but Sonny hated men. Somewhere, long ago, some man had abused him and he retreated from them, and once, when Dan picked up a stick that had been lying on the ground, the pony bolted to the far end of the field and stood shivering, revealing something of his history. Dan had been unable to catch him, and it was Lisa who coaxed him back to sanity. But he had not yet allowed Philip to stay on his back.

He hunched himself neatly, put down his head and bucked his rider to the ground. Dan sighed, as Sonny moved out of reach. It never did to buy an animal in a hurry and he should not have let Philip's importunity rule him. But they all missed Beau. The pony had been part of their lives for so long; was older than either of the children and had had endearing ways, adoring ice-cream, stealing it whenever he saw a hand holding a cornet, coming to the gate and whinnying whenever Dan or Anna passed, asking for a caress, for attention, never, in all his life, showing any sign of ill temper.

Sonny was a challenge. He was also a nuisance, and apt to bully Tarquin, who bore it patiently, an old man tolerating the younger generation. Tarquin stood back meekly when Sonny stole his hay; the pony had been ill kept and was making up for years of bad feeding. At least he looked better than when he had come to them.

Dan went back to the house. Anna had made the soup and served it on the counter beside the sink. Their furniture would come in the morning. Meanwhile there were two big padded window-seats upstairs on which they could lie, borrowing the children's sleeping-bags.

Anna put Smoke and her kittens beside the radiator in the big room. She could not be let out for several days, lest she wandered, but as long as the kittens were here, there was no fear of losing her. If she were chased by a dog, or alarmed by some unfamiliar noise, she might well miss her way. And there were frequent cars along the lane. Compton Hall stood at the end of a private road that led nowhere. There had been little traffic. This was very different. The lane connected two busy main roads, and in the rush hour, drivers used it as a short-cut. The cat would be at risk.

Dan took hay to the horses. He patted Tarquin and watched Sonny skitter to the far side of the field. The pony was like Bracken in colouring, the pony of Dan's youth. Dan had been attracted by the similarity in appearance, but there all likeness ended. Dan's first pony had been a gentle creature, not a wild neglected beast, distrustful of everyone.

The evening stretched before them. There was nothing to do. Anna walked down the lane and looked across at the rash of red brick houses on the other side of the main road. She was glad they could not be seen from her windows. They crowded against her eyes so that she longed for the space of her lost garden, for the vista beyond to May Hill, rising tree-clad and lovely against the skyline, blocking the further view.

Here she looked out over flat fields to winter-bare trees, and the land lacked all character. No slope and swing and sweep of hillock, no rise to the sky; only endless fields, sparse hedges, and no birds anywhere. If only she could go back . . .

Dan had found his own solution and walked down the lane to the cowfield. They were Friesians, not a patch on his herd. He looked them over hungrily. Land hunger. Cattle hunger, a fever that was rising inside him. He could never settle down to life without animals, but now that all debts were paid and the cottages were bought and altered, there was little enough money left and he was too old to start again. He had invested the capital that remained to bring in some income.

Anger needled him. They had no right to thrust him out of his home. If only he could fight them; could punch and kick and savage; he needed action, and there was no action possible. He needed Anna but she had retreated in misery and when he went back she was sitting on the window-seat upstairs, a kitten on her knees, staring out of the window.

Night time was penance.

Anna lay listening to the sounds in the cottage. Unfamiliar sounds. The hoot of a diesel train running along a railway line nearby; the unnerving roar of an aeroplane taking off over the house. She had not realised that the airport was so close. There were plane sounds all night, waking her from uneasy dozes, breaking into dreams of their old farmhouse, lying empty under the sky, with the bulldozers moving towards it.

Moonlight barred the ceiling. The window was in the wrong place. She hated the unfamiliar room. An owl called, and that at least was familiar. Yet, in spite of the noises, everything was dead. No rustle of cattle in the sheds beyond them. No stamp of horses in the stable. Tarquin and Sonny Boy were too far away to hear. No barking from a dog. She would never grow used to it. Never. And, lying there awake, she hated Dan, who had given her all she ever wanted and then let them deprive her of it.

It was a little easier next morning when the furniture van arrived, and there was need to make decisions; to bring the chintz-covered chairs into the big room, already carpeted; to arrange the books; to put the ornaments on the high shelf that Dan had fixed above the picture rail; the stag that Philip had brought back when he went on a school trip to Spain; Lisa's collection of china horses that was added to every year by her friends. Anna fingered them; little white copies of Ming horses; a frisking colt; a big Shire; a horse that might have been modelled on Tarquin a little Arab, a real treasure, sculpted by a modern artist in wood, given to Lisa by her godmother.

There was a painting of Compton Hall, dating from the early nineteenth century. Dan looked at it, and hid it in a cupboard. It was too soon to live with that. He fixed hooks in the big living-room for the three hunting prints that had hung in their old kitchen, and Anna put the shaggy rug down beside the radiator. It looked wrong and she longed for an open fire where logs would blaze at night, but Dan had elected to have central heating installed and save work.

What on earth would they do with their time, Anna wondered, and desolation swept over her again as Smoke came into the room, the kittens running behind her, and settled at once on the familiar rug, close to the warm radiator, and began to purr. It must be wonderful to be a cat, Anna thought.

Dan went out to the kitchen that evening to cook a meal, unable to reconcile himself to idleness. It took such a little time to arrange the rooms. They had sold most of the furniture; there was no space for it here. Anna had kept the big old kitchen dresser. That now had pride of place against the living-room wall, its black wood sharply contrasted with the white paint. There were the rosettes awarded to the cattle; red and blue and green and yellow; firsts and seconds, thirds and fourths; there was the cup that Lisetta had carried off in the last year's gymkhana, and Anna's own cups, won soon after Philip was born, in the leisurely days when money had value and Anna had had a housekeeper.

When they had eaten, Dan went to look for the horses' tack, and cleaned it until it shone, rubbing savagely, venting all his anger on the leather, so that it gleamed when he had finished as it had not gleamed for years. The two saddles reflected his shadow. Smoke watched with interest and the kittens teased at the rag he was using and played with his shoelaces, and Anna, coming into the little tack-room that had once been a scullery, took up reins and bridles and worked alongside, finding relief in busy hands.

'Let's explore,' Dan suggested, and they went out

together into the dark and down the lane, stopping to pat Tarquin, while Sonny watched distrustfully, but let Anna stroke his nose when Dan walked on. The grazing was poor; the land not half so rich as their Cotswold field, and the horses would need far more extra feed here. It was a small niggling worry. Anna had no idea how they would manage on a fixed income. Before, there had always been something to sell; milk and eggs and calves and harvests. Money coming in all the time. January had always been planning time. Now there were no plans.

A plane swept into the sky, wing and tail lights flashing, and Anna turned her head, hearing the thunder of Sonny's hooves. He wasn't used to planes. He fled to the far corner of the field, but Tarquin plodded after him, and the two bodies merged. The old horse was never afraid and he seemed to understand the pony's need.

There was nowhere to go and no one to see. They turned back and Anna walked slowly down the garden. The corner of it was marshy, filled with reeds, and clogged with last year's dead rushes. The moon was reflected in the water.

'We could make an ornamental lake,' Dan said. It would be something to do.

'And have ducks.' There was a flicker of interest in Anna's voice as she visualised the busy waddling creatures, quacking and quarrelling, livening the deadness.

'Muscovy ducks,' Dan said, the words a promise. He had always liked them but somehow never got around to keeping them.

Perhaps there was a future after all.

CHAPTER FOUR

Snow lay deep covering the wintry fields. There were azaleas in every nearby garden, promising future colour, a constant reminder of all that Anna had lost. There was no room for them here. And she had not wanted to carry memories so vivid into a new life. Nothing must remind her of Compton. Memory was unbearable.

When the snow melted Dan began to work. He fenced the ground and reinforced the hedges round the horses' field. Tarquin, although he was gelded, had too many memories of the days when he had enjoyed his pride, and would escape to flirt with any mare within smelling distance, and smelling distance was a very long way. And wandering horses would not be welcome here, where most of the homes were suburban and animals had no place.

There had always been visitors to Compton Hall, coming in to the big kitchen, calling out to announce their arrival, sure of a welcome, of a cup of coffee, and a little of Anna's time, and there had always been conversation; talk of cattle and horses and dogs; of pigs and of poultry and the summer shows, and the children's jumping competitions, and the pony club meetings.

There had always been children too, racing in and out, coming to see the new litter of pigs, the chicks in the barn, the pups in the stable, the new foal in the big meadow, where Syrena had lived for so long. Children borrowing the ponies; children coming to tea with Philip or Lisetta, adoring Anna's farmhouse spreads of new baked bread and cut-and-come-again currant cake, and sponges light as cats' breath, and junkets, and fruit picked from the garden, and thick Jersey cream.

It seemed a waste of time cooking for just herself and Dan. If only the children had come too, but it wouldn't have been sensible. If only she had something to do with the endless days. It was useless trying to help Dan. The land was sick and sour and hard to dig, and he daily regretted his fine Cotswold soil and the richness of their old garden. This was three parts clay; was waterlogged and had never, in all its years, been fed with any kind of fertiliser. If Anna came to help, Dan relieved his irritation by snapping at her, and she began to haunt the horse field and occupy herself with gentling Sonny, coaxing him to come to her; to stand while she groomed him and cleaned the tangles from his mane and tail; to accept pony nuts from her hand.

Tarquin was easy to groom and she spent hours on the old horse until his coat gleamed with brushing and he looked better than he had looked for years.

But it was not enough.

The days stretched endlessly and pointlessly in front of her, and the people who passed never spoke, not even when she smiled. Children came to look at the horses, but if she approached them, they ran away.

She began to think she had moved into hostile country, until the first day of February when she decided that Smoke's kittens must go to new homes, and went to put a notice in the pet shop window, and walked down the lane to explore the shopping streets more thoroughly.

She had not visited this part of their new territory before.

Chadleigh had been a small village twenty-five years before, a sprawl of fields and lanes and narrow streets. Now its character had been lost in redevelopment. It had grown to a nondescript place, though some of the charming old houses still survived

31

among the shopping precincts and brash garages and multi-storey office blocks. Many earlier buildings had been pulled down to make way for glass-fronted modern shops with names like Zingo and Whizzkid and Pete's Pet Place, which was not, as she had expected, a pet shop at all, but a little boutique selling the most extraordinary clothes that Anna had ever seen.

She turned up a side road, and here the old village remained; the ancient little bow-fronted sweet shop, where a big Alsatian barked at her from the window; the tiny street of Elizabethan cottages, ending in a cobbled yard where once carriages had turned. The stables were now maisonettes, bright and pretty, and gay with painted window boxes in which were yellow daffodils, just coming into bloom. They must have been forced and planted out. It was too early for daffodils.

The pet shop was on the opposite side of the road. Anna crossed, holding the card that she had written. There were other cards in the window. One, in particular, startled her into attention.

S.O.S.

Wanted, urgently, home for bitch about to whelp and two in-milk goats. Owner's wife in hospital.

Two goats, in milk. And a bitch about to whelp. And no one to care for them. Anna pushed the door open and walked inside. She had been a farmer's wife too long and here were animals that needed her, if only no one had claimed them. She was almost afraid to ask.

The address she was given was in a village four miles away. Anna went home and started off again in the station wagon, not even telling Dan where she was going. He might protest. They had agreed that animals could not be part of their lives again; that they would have to go carefully without any extra money coming in; that they must discover how to live on a fixed income before they branched out in any way.

But she couldn't bear to think of animals being neglected, or in need of a home. There was room for the goats in the horse field and she loved goats' milk, and besides then they needn't buy cows' milk and it would be an economy. The goats would pay for themselves and she could get them in kid and sell the kids. She might be able to sell the milk. There would be enough money coming in to pay for their keep.

And she could sell the puppies. She shut her eyes to the fact that she knew nothing about the bitch; not even the breed. That could wait. She would have a dog about the place again and it was lonely in the lane and she needed a guard dog. The cottage was called Setter's Dene, and if that didn't mean there had been dogs there once, she didn't know what it did mean. And the lane was Billy's Lane. For the first time she wondered who Billy had been, and if he had lived in one of the two cottages.

If only the goats and the bitch were still there. She needed occupation. She needed animals. She couldn't live without them and it was useless trying. And Dan needed animals too, no matter what they had decided.

For the first time since she had heard that the motorway was coming through their land and across the site of Compton Hall, Anna felt hope rising. Life was a little less bleak.

She turned into a narrow lane. The pet shop owner had drawn a map for her, and it was easy to find her way. There was a small public house at the corner, white painted, with a dark sign. The Roosting Peacock. Beyond it was her destination.

The cottage was built of honey-coloured stone. Mullioned windows reflected the sun. The yellow thatch was newly finished, the ladders used by the workmen being removed as she parked her car at the little wooden gate. A cobbled path led to a thick oak door, which stood open. A black cat sunned itself on the step.

The man who came to the door was very old. He was toothless and anxious. Once he had been tall and heavily built, but now he was stooped and his clothes hung loosely on him. His brown eyes looked at Anna, worry in his glance.

'I came about the goats and the bitch,' she said.

'You'd take them?' he asked, and motioned her inside and broke into urgent speech.

'Do you really know about goats and whelping bitches? I don't want them to go to just anyone . . . I mean, they've been family. Only the old woman's ill . . . it's her heart, the doctor says, and she's got to give them up when she comes home. I wouldn't want them to go to someone who didn't know how to look after them. And they've been pets, real pets.'

'We had a farm,' Anna said. 'They've knocked it down to build the new motorway.'

Bitterness marred her voice.

'That's bad.' There was concern in the old man's eyes. 'But at least you'll know how we feel.'

Anna nodded. She knew, only too well.

'The bitch is in the kitchen,' the old man said. He led the way down a narrow passage carpeted with a brown haircord runner edged with gold. The walls closed in, bright with red roses and improbable blue tulips. A hatstand took up much of the space, a curly-legged table beside it on which stood a china statuette of a woman dressed in long blue robes, riding a bright red horse.

The kitchen was warm and friendly, a tiny room in which a fire blazed cosily; another cat curled in a wicker chair that was bright with scarlet cushions. Red curtains hung at the tiny window and all the paint was red. The bitch lifted her head.

Anna was lost as the animal looked up.

She was a pedigree Alsatian, beautifully bred and even with the pups distorting her body, she was elegant. Her gentle eyes gazed at Anna and she growled softly, a warning rumble deep in her throat.

'Hush, girl,' the old man said, and the long tail wagged once, and the bitch lay still.

'There's plenty as don't like Alsatians,' the old man said. 'But Zelie is gentle. Gentle as they come. And so's the sire of them pups. They're good pups. We were going to sell them, but that don't matter now. All I want is that she goes to someone who'll treat her right. She's a house pet, not a kennel dog. And my son trained her. She's a good little worker and them's her cups. For Beauty. And for Obedience,' he added. 'My son's in the Navy now. So she doesn't work any more.'

Anna looked at the cups ranged on the dresser. 'How old is she?' she asked.

'Four years old. This is her second litter. She won't be no trouble. She's a good little mother. Never puts a paw wrong.'

'I'll take her,' Anna said. 'On one condition.'

The old man looked at her, misery in his face. 'What condition?' he asked.

'That the pups remain yours. I'll sell them for you, and send you the money. It'd not be fair, otherwise.'

He shook his head.

'Free to a good home, I said, and I meant it,' he said emphatically.

'Then we go halves, or I pay for the bitch,' Anna said. 'I'm a farmer's wife. I know what she's cost you to keep and I know her stud fee. I'll only take her if you agree, and I'm buying the goats; you can't just give them away.'

'I wouldn't sell my children,' the old man said.

'Please,' Anna said. 'I can't take them without. And you can use the money to buy something nice for your wife if you don't need it.'

'They're out there,' he said, and led the way into a little orchard where pear blossom would soon begin to colour the trees. The two goats were tethered, cropping the grass. Both were white, with long wise faces.

'That one's Heidi, and that one's Jezebel,' the old man said. 'Heidi's in kid. It's her first, so it's as well you know about animals. When will you take them?'

'Now,' Anna said recklessly, the thought of animals about the place an excitement; there would be animal chores again. She would have the goats to milk and the bitch to feed, and the bitch would have to learn to know her. She would be sad to leave her owners, but she would settle, given time.

The old man brought the bitch to the station wagon and put her inside, in the front of the car. Anna was aware of anxious eyes that grew more anxious when he returned with bed and plate and collar and leads. He brought the two goats out and put them in the back of the wagon, behind the dog guard. Anna had written the cheque. She shut the door and watched the old man walk away, defeat in the line of his shoulders. He slammed the door, and she knew that he could not bear to look round and see her drive off. The bitch curled up on the floor in front of the empty passenger seat, her eyes forlorn.

Anna let in the clutch. Now she had Dan to face.

There was no sign of him when she reached the cottage. She drove into the little yard and closed the gate. She would have to put the goats in the shed until Dan could tether them; and come to think of it, there was no tether and no rope and tomorrow was Sunday. They would have to stay indoors. Goats could jump and these too might well run away from strangers. But when Anna went into the shed she found that the door would not shut. The hinges were faulty.

She left the goats in the car, and coaxed the bitch indoors. Zelie followed her, wary, sniffing at the kitchen floor, sniffing at Anna's outstretched hand, watching as feeding dish and water bowl were brought inside and the cans of dogfood and the meal that the old man had handed over. Anna began to prepare a feed; once she had fed the animal, some confidence would be established. Smoke put her head round the kitchen door when she heard the tin rattle against the plate, saw the Alsatian and swore and fled, chivvying her kittens to safety.

Only then did Anna remember that she had forgotten to arrange to have her card put in the pet shop window. She would have to go back again. It was still in her handbag.

And there would be problems with Smoke, as she would defend her kittens from a strange dog. And Sonny hated dogs too. He had never seen a goat, and they would have to graze in the field with the horses. It had been so easy at the old farm, with plenty of space, and barns for the cats, who spent much of the year outside, and room for the dogs, and so many fields that the animals could easily be separated. She had never been used to so small a scale. Had never realised until now that lack of space was such a problem.

The bitch followed her anxiously, afraid of being alone, worried by unfamiliarity. Anna took Smoke and the kittens upstairs and shut them in the spare bedroom that had been made from one of the two vast bathrooms. She came down again to find the Alsatian standing patiently, watching her from glowing brown eyes, noting every movement, totally unafraid. Zelie had known nothing but kindness all through her life. It never occurred to her that people could harm her. When Anna sat down in the big chintz-covered chair and picked up a book, the Alsatian sighed deeply and dropped to the floor, her head on Anna's foot. She needed reassurance.

And Anna needed the bitch's trust. Those pups were not far off birth. She would need to prepare for

37

them. A good big whelping box with room for the pups; and where in the world would she put them? Suppose there were nine or more? Nine tiny pups were all very well, but there wasn't room for nine seven-week-old pups to tumble on the floor and mark the new carpets, and there was nowhere outside where they could sleep.

Anna picked up her book. Problems could be solved, and the need to think of animals was already restoring her, was making life more normal, was easing the ache caused by leaving her old home. If they could build a new life here . . . perhaps there was hope, after all. Her fingers stroked the hard head, fondled the firm ears, smoothed the thick fur. She could breed dogs; she knew little enough about the business, but like everything else, it could be learned, and perhaps she could breed a champion, an all-time great dog that would leave his mark on his progeny. Zelie was beautiful enough for any judge to award her prizes; she had a long history of winning; Anna had seen the cups and rosettes and she had the pedigree and even she knew enough to recognise some of the names. A neighbour of hers in the Cotswolds had bred Alsatians. Mollie always talked dog talk, and lived in a world apart.

As dusk shadowed the garden, Anna began to plan for the first time for weeks, finding balm in constructive thought. Only what was Dan going to say when he came home and found three new members of the family and two of them about to give birth?

She waited, wishing he would hurry home, wondering where he had gone. Had he worried because she had taken the car without warning him; had he been afraid that her misery would drive her to do something stupid? She should have told him, but it was too late now. She could only switch on the lights and watch the gathering dusk, and see Tarquin put his wise old head over the hedge and gaze into the room, apparently fascinated by human appurtenances. Sonny was too small to see over the hedge. He was a tiny pony, delicately made, and now that he was putting flesh on hungry bones, was very pretty.

Anna had been sleeping badly for weeks. She dozed in the warm room, for the first time at ease, with the dog beside her. She was wakened by a low-pitched growl and a clatter of hooves. She jumped up, startled. It was dark outside, but Dan was there, and he had two ponies with him. Zelie was at the window, growling at the noise outside.

Anna went to the back door.

'Look at this!' Dan was explosive, his dark brows drawn together, his expression furious. He was standing beside a light chestnut pony which trembled violently. There were sores all over the small beast's back. Its brown eyes were terrified. It was a little Shetland with long tail and shaggy fur and thinner than even Sonny had been.

The second pony was a grey, a Welsh mountain pony with a kind face. Its body was gaunt and its mane and tail tangled and matted. It was lame on one foreleg.

'I found them in a field down the lane,' Dan said. 'No extra feed. Hardly any grass on the ground. And look at these girth galls. I went to the farm to find out who owned them. The farmer's been complaining for months. Some man bought them for his daughters last Christmas, but they don't know as much about horses as I know about Egyptian history and that's precious little. I paid the owner thirty pounds. The kids never ride them. We can get them into decent condition and maybe Joe will buy one for Susy for her next birthday. Their names are Suntan and Razzle.'

Anna looked at her husband helplessly, stifling a desire to laugh. Their niece had been clamouring for a pony for years and Dan knew perfectly well that her mother would never allow it. They had two more ponies of their own to live with Tarquin and Sonny. No doubt about that.

'I know we said no more animals,' Dan began, and then the pent-up feelings of weeks of misery broke in a tide over Anna's head and hysteria choked her, so that she leaned on the kitchen table, seeing the light streaming through the open door on to the ponies' bewildered heads, and laughed helplessly, unable to stop herself, laughing until tears suddenly poured down her face and she had to run to the bathroom and bathe her eyes with cold water while Dan, baffled, led the newcomers into the garden and turned them loose, ensuring that the gate was tied with rope so that no one could let the little beasts free. No use putting them with Tarquin and Sonny until he was sure they would accept them and not bully them. They would half kill one another if they'd a mind.

He took out hay and pony nuts, and watched the ponies feed ravenously. From behind him came the bleat of a goat. He turned his head, curious. Surely there were no goats on the nearby farm. He hadn't seen any and he had looked over all the stock, envy riding him. Envy of another man who had his livelihood at his fingertips and lived in the home where he had been born and had land to give to his sons.

The goat bleated again.

Dan went to the car. Surely it could not have come from there? He opened the door and looked inside disbelief in his eyes. Both goats had settled on the straw that Anna had put for them behind the dog guard, unable to think of any other place that was safe. The swelling lines of the kid showed only too clearly. Dan closed the door and went inside.

He was greeted by a loud growl, as Zelie flew forward, anxious to defend her new mistress from the intruder. Anna called sharply and the bitch stopped, abashed.

Anna looked at her husband. His mouth began to twitch, and within moments the two of them were laughing helplessly, unable to stop, lightheaded at the thought of having animals to care for again, of having live creatures all around them again, of beginning in a small way to live a more natural existence, with the needs of beasts of fill the endless hours, and the problems of housing them already occupying Dan's mind as Anna dished the meal and brought it into the livingroom, where they sat in companionable silence and watched Zelie settle herself on the rug again.

'When are her pups due?' Dan asked.

'In about a week,' Anna said. 'She needs a whelping box; and where are we going to put her? There's nowhere outside.'

'That's easy,' Dan said, and when he had eaten he rolled back the carpet from the floor near the french windows. 'The room's plenty big enough to spare space for her. I'll soon knock up a box for her. And she can get outside through the windows.'

'Make it big,' Anna said, not thinking, and Dan laughed again.

'Anyone'd think I'd never handled an in-whelp bitch in my life before,' he said, and Anna suddenly remembered that before their marriage Dan had bred and trained his own Border collies. They had intended to begin again but the cattle dominated their time and somehow they never had.

Dan licked his fingers and Zelie went to him and sniffed his clothes. He smelled of horse. She liked horses and she liked men. The old man and his son had worked with her and played with her, and she trusted them, knowing that they would never harm her. She leaned against Dan's knee, and he took out his pipe and filled it, and relaxed in the arm-chair.

There was a small stir at the door.

Anna opened it and found the boldest of the kittens outside. Little black Soot, with his green eyes

41

and blue tinged fur, and a Siamese yowl that told of odd ancestry. Goodness knew what Tom had mated Smoke, but he hadn't been pure Siamese or the kittens would have shown it. Only Smoke herself had some Siamese ancestry.

'Quiet,' Anna said, as the Alsatian moved. Zelie dropped back on to the rug, and the kitten sidled across the room, curious. He had never seen a dog before. His back arched instinctively as he caught her smell, and he spat. Anna picked him up and gentled him. He loved Anna and curled close, snuggling into her lap, but watched the dog anxiously, ready to run if Zelie moved.

A moment later Smoke raced into the room, leaped to Anna's lap, grabbed her kitten by the scruff of his neck and ran from the room, Soot dangling from her jaws, voicing his indignation.

'I'll fix the shed door and put the goats inside before I go to bed,' Dan said, laughing at the cat's abrupt exit. 'And you'll have to buy some provender for the goats in the morning. I'll give them pony nuts and carrots. When were they last fed?'

Anna had forgotten to ask. She held the shed door steady while Dan mended the hinges, and spread straw across the floor. Dan had already cleaned it, intending to use it as store room for the horses' feed. She brought the goats inside and watched them settle, at ease in their new home and apparently unworried, the pair of them company for one another, unbothered by their change of owner.

That night Anna lay listening, hearing the new ponies moving about the garden, hooves striking hard when they crossed the path. She heard one whinny and Tarquin answer, and one of the goats bleated.

Zelie had followed her upstairs and curled on the floor beside the bed. She was better off there; if she began to whelp unexpectedly, Anna would know at once and be able to help her to the whelping box.

42

If only she didn't whelp early, before it was ready. That would create problems.

Outside the window an owl hooted. Anna turned to face the dark, seeing the fretted outline of trees against the skyline, the shape of a church steeple, that she had never noticed before, in the distance, the shadows of clouds beyond the newly risen moon.

'It's like beginning again,' Dan said sleepily from his own bed. 'I should have known . . .' His voice tailed off sleepily, and he never finished the sentence, but Anna finished it for him, knowing that he meant that life, for them, was impossible without animals about them, and that new interests were beginning and that perhaps, one day, Setter's Dene would also be a home.

CHAPTER FIVE

Anna could not believe that a dog could make so much difference to life. She was never alone. Zelie followed her everywhere, anxious not to lose this owner too. The Alsatian was a shadow, padding at heel, lying beside Anna's chair, coming out to the car, jumping inside as soon as Anna picked up the keys, so that she wondered if the bitch hoped that she would be taken to her old home rather than stay here among strangers.

They were both exiles, Anna thought, as she walked down the little lane, Zelie sniffing at the grass verge, identifying the scents of other animals. She kept close to Anna, and when strangers passed, came at once to heel, her eyes watchful, protecting her mistress. Her guard sense was very strong, and already her new owner was an ally, a part of Zelie's life, and no one would ever be allowed to touch her except Dan, whom the bitch recognised as family.

Smoke was still very wary and never entered the room when Zelie was there, but the kittens had already accepted the Alsatian, and one morning Dan called Anna to come and look. She found that the whelping box was finished and Zelie was lying inside, as if well aware of its function, with four kittens tucked up against her, well soaked from the ministrations of her busy tongue. Soot was with them, but he had stretched himself on Zelie's warm flank and lay there with eyes closed, purring blissfully, flexing his tiny claws in and out of her fur. The old man was right. Zelie was a born mother.

Anna had bought a book about bloodlines in the Alsatian and was studying it, with Zelie's pedigree form beside her. She was fascinated to discover how many of Zelie's ancestors were champions who had influenced the breed. No doubt at all that Zelie should have splendid pups.

The makings were there, dating from the long-ago German influence and the more modern British champions that had formed the basis for the present-day dog, with his noble head and wise eyes, erect ears and alert expression, lovely gait and long tail that seemed a continuation of his elegant body, sweeping to a satisfying line that held the attention. Zelie was beautifully marked, her head and shoulders black, her underparts gold. Her coat was in fine condition. She had been well cared for, and the veterinary surgeon that Anna took her to see could find no possible source of worry.

'She's in splendid shape,' he said.

'They should be wonderful pups,' Anna said at breakfast two days before they were due.

Dan was superstitious. He always touched wood

44

and never walked under ladders; you never knew. And you never spoke of possible triumphs. That way, they never came to pass.

'Never count your apples . . .' he said hastily and, Anna finished the sentence for him.

'Till the blossom is set. As your grandfather used to say. Dan, nothing more can go wrong. We've had enough bad luck to last a lifetime. Losing Compton Hall was the most awful thing that could have happened.'

'We're together and alive and the children are well,' Dan said. 'Have you forgotten that?'

There were worse things, Anna thought suddenly and bleakly. Only you pushed them out of mind, not wanting to dwell on them, or to tempt providence.

She pushed the thought away. It was time to put bedding in the box for Zelie. Dan had made it good and strong, out of new wood with three sides high and the fourth adjustable so that Zelie could step in and out easily, but it could be arranged to keep the pups from wandering while they were too small. Anna brought in a pile of newspapers, pulled them apart and put the separate sheets, curled in loose crumpled masses, in the box. Zelie knew at once what she had to do, and the whole morning was punctuated by the sound of tearing paper as she shredded it for her bed. Her time was very near.

Never count your apples . . .

The words haunted Anna so that she was suddenly afraid to leave the bitch alone. Suppose the pups wouldn't come, or were dead? Suppose the bitch died while she was whelping? Suppose Smoke got into the room and attacked the litter? They would be so very small and helpless. She began to close the door every time she left the room, and every time Zelie padded towards it and whined to be let out and to come into the kitchen or into the yard, where she could be near Anna.

And there was a problem with the new ponies too.

45

Little Suntan, gentle and charming, was hated by both Sonny and Tarquin. Sonny bit him and Tarquin chased him from end to end of the field, warning him away, resenting the intrusion. It was impossible to put them together so that Suntan stayed in the garden with Razzle and put his head round the kitchen door and stole any food that Anna had forgotten to put away. The carrots vanished and all the bread was apt to disappear too. Dan had bought two tethering pins and lengths of nylon rope and the goats were staked in the garden. It was a good job there were two acres of ground. Dan worked on Suntan daily, cleaning and dressing the sores, and the little animal soon learned the time of day and came trotting for attention, more affectionate than any pony that Dan had ever known. Razzle was jealous and vied for attention, and rubbed his head against Dan's arm. They were an amusing pair.

The days had point again. Animals were salvation. Anna, reading the book on Alsatian breeding, noting the inheritance of characteristics such as temperament, and shyness, and various working abilities, began to realise that human breeding carried inherited characteristics too. Maybe much of the difficulty in industry was due to the fact that men no longer worked in the old ways with skills that had been fostered and handed down, generation by generation, through the centuries. It was so easy to follow; Britain was an island, with sea all around it, and sailing was a national pastime; the love of water was inherited through centuries of fishermen ancestors, through ancestors who went to sea with Nelson; or, longer back, with Raleigh and with Drake. So that thousands of Britons longed to go to sea and spend their free time sailing.

And the need to explore, coming down through the ages; and above all the land hunger that in many men was so strong that they salved it in their gardens, putting into the tiny plots all the energy that their forebears had used on their farms.

Both she and Dan had farmers in their ancestry. Cattle and horse breeders, men to whom animals were more important than anything else in life. As she watched over Zelie, Anna suddenly remembered her grandfather never speaking to anyone when he was watching over a foaling mare, his thoughts in the stable, where he checked constantly, even though the headman was reliable. And Grandfather had been present at every birth, right up to his last year, when at eighty-seven he had gone out, in spite of a heavy cold, to Verity, who had got herself in foal by mistake when she was much too old. Grandfather had adored Verity and when she died foaling he seemed to lose all heart and had taken to his own bed and died three weeks later, not caring any longer about the farm or the other horses.

And Dan's father had been the same, as excited over his newest calf as if it had been the first, planning for its future, intending to breed the best Friesian of all time; the cow with the highest milk yield; the cow with the best calves; the cow that would win the highest award at the dairy shows. With so many dedicated ancestors how could they ever hope to settle down to a suburban life without farm creatures about them?

Anna couldn't wait for Zelie's pups. Excitement mastered her. She fed the bitch two meals a day, adding calcium and an occasional raw egg; giving her milk to drink, cutting down on cereal to make the meals less bulky; watching over her every second lest she ran into the garden and whelped outside.

There was no time to be lonely now. Anna was glad the children were away, as the bitch could whelp in peace. It was always hard to keep Philip from brooding over new young animals. Lisetta was very good, but some of her friends were impossible and wanted to maul young stock. One child had been thoroughly kicked by Syrena when she tried to stroke the foal that had been born only two days before. After that, Anna had banned all visitors until the newcomers were older and the mothers less possessive. Modern children had no training in respect for beasts. It was a wonder that more of them didn't get hurt.

The day before Zelie was due to whelp, Dan offered to watch her and Anna left the bitch for a couple of hours, while her husband worked at his accounts. She took Tarquin and rode down the lane. She had not yet explored the far end beyond the bridle path, and she was becoming curious. She had known every inch of the land around Compton Hall, had known the surge of colour in the autumn beech-woods, the new soft promise of green on the branches in spring, the lie and drift of snow, white and glittering, when winter snarled over the land and held the world in thrall.

She knew the rise of May Hill and the cloudy trees that clothed its slopes and the lift and swell of the ground and the yellow crops and the brown of the fields new turned under plough. She knew the lazy twine of the river, the summer banks edged with a tumble of colour from the flowers that rioted, yellow and scarlet and blue vying with the sudden flash of the kingfisher diving from a willow branch.

Here she only saw flat fields and the bare trees; they were so very late to leaf. The hedges promised flowers very soon, the buds hidden and secret, a glint of white between their teeth, a shimmer of green softening the stark branches. There was one precocious yellow colts-foot deep in the grass at the hedge bottom. A squirrel flashed over the road and lifted himself lightly into a tree and watched the horse pass beneath him. Anna was aware of the bright dark eyes and the curled thick furry tail. There was a drey above the animal, a tangle of twigs and dead leaves wedged clumsily into the fork

of two branches. There should soon be young. Anna
liked squirrels, though Dan called them tree rats and
complained about their destructiveness. The rhodo-
dendrons at Compton Hall had always suffered.

And with that thought came a return of desolation. There would soon have been a sweep of colour
on the shrubs beyond her kitchen window, bloom
massed on bushes that had been collected for genera-
tions. There would have been twenty new calves to
look forward to in the late spring, and the new foal
from the brood mare they had been unable to keep.
No room for a brood mare at Setter's Dene. Anna
rode on, looking over the bleak flat fields that were
soaked and muddy with recent rain. Did it always
rain in Cheshire, she wondered. The air was still, the
sky a flat expanse of dull grey cloud, and not even
the thought of Zelie's pups could rouse Anna's
spirits.

If only she were riding on May Hill; if only she
were returning to Compton Hall; if only the bridle
path led to the village of honey-coloured stone cottages that had warmed themselves for centuries
under a soft Cotswold sun; if only the accents she
heard were familiar and not the harsher North
Country sounds with their odd vowels. The other
morning she had gone to look for a shop which someone had told her was in the centre of the village
street, a shop owned by a man named Gunn. She had
asked for Gunn's and been met with blank stares.

It was not till the fourth request that she received
a helpful reply. The man had stared at her, and then
had placed her, at once, as a stranger to the locality.

'You mean Goon's,' he had said, pronouncing the
double oo sound as it was pronounced in "book' and
had pointed the shop out to her, making Anna feel
as if she had come to another country and not merely
another county; as if she were a total stranger in an
alien world, unable to communicate at all. She had
gone home bleakly, longing for someone to call at the

door, to come in and share a pot of tea and a gossip over biscuits, but there was no one near. How did one get to know people in a new place, she wondered. It was bad enough to lose your home without losing companionship as well. If only Ellie were here, coming in joyous over a bargain in her shopping, or bringing the latest pup from the kennels to see her. Ellie had bred West Highland terriers; gay little dogs who adored coming with their breeder to explore the farm and make friends with Anna's animals.

The bridle path led out on to a narrow main road. Beyond the road an RAC sign pointed to Sarvan Hall. Beyond the sign the bridle path continued.

Anna crossed the road and followed the path. She rode between newly cut hedges, hacked gracelessly by a machine. The raw wood was exposed to the chilly air and the tops of the branches still lay in untidy heaps on the field side of the hedge. There were no animals in the fields. No birds. No beasts. She had come into a world that seemed as sterile as the concrete jungle of the towns.

Tarquin stopped, startled, facing two immense wrought iron gates, hung between stone pillars. There was a small postern gate beyond them. On the far side was a gravelled drive, edged by lawns where a man was sweeping. A bank of azaleas, promising vivid colour later, was planted against the side of a long, low black-and-white timbered house. Anna caught her breath. Someone had loved this place, as much as she had loved her old home. It lay serene, as untroubled by the passage of the centuries as the grounds around it.

The old man looked up.

'You can bring the horse inside if you want to look round the gardens,' he said. 'Only walk him, please, miss, and keep off the gravel. It's newly swept all round and takes a power of keeping. The azaleas will be a rare sight soon, and there's more in the garden beyond the house. You must come back later and see them in bloom.' He had noticed the expression in Anna's eyes.

'Is it all right to go round there with my horse?' Anna asked.

'Bless you, yes. This place was built for horses. The children from the riding school bring their ponies here. It's quiet and there's miles of paths; there's nearly five hundred acres of grounds round the house, and the old Squire likes to see the kids about. He lost both his sons in the war. It's lonely for him. This is National Trust property now. He just has a little flat at the end of the house. No one to leave it to, more's the pity.'

'Have you worked here long?' Anna asked.

'All my life, except for the First World War. Fought in the trenches there. Was in the Sappers. I had an old mule in those days and slept between his legs to keep warm. Old Misty; grey as them clouds, and as placid as a cow chewing her cud. It was a good life here, in them days. None of this rush and hurry. There were people with time to listen. Nobody listens, not now. And not to old men. Better dead, the young ones reckon, put them out of their misery. Forgetting one day they'll be old too.'

Anna nodded, unable to think of an appropriate answer. Nobody had time. Rush and bustle and mind your own business and all it got you was loneliness and a gravelled path to sweep at the end of your days. She pulled herself together, prodded Tarquin into motion, and walked away between the trees that grew thickly in the grass.

She paused, looking down. It was hilly here; only small hills but at least the landscape was shaped and broken; beyond her a waterfall trickled gently over a rocky cliff into a small man-made grotto. Azaleas grew on either side, massed together. They would, in a few weeks, be brilliantly coloured. She could have looked all day.

But she would have to get back. She walked on,

leading Tarquin along the lawn at the side of the house, and turned into gardens that were alight with colour; colour from winter heathers just coming into bloom; in summer there must be colour everywhere, Anna thought, looking at the well-stocked flower-beds and massed shrubs. The house rose behind them, its outline gracious, a memory of a past when men had been proud to raise buildings that were lovely to look at and showed the craftsman's skill in every corner.

'You like my house,' a voice said behind her, and Anna turned to see a small man, his hair white, his dark eyes glitteringly alive in a face so wrinkled that it was difficult to imagine his age. She had never seen anyone so old.

'I'm ninety-eight,' he said, proud of his long years. 'Lived through more changes than any one of my ancestors, I imagine. You travel the right way. Everyone dashes off in cars these days, and they never see the country. My riding days are over, but I always had a horse, until I was turned eighty, when the doctor said I was too old to ride. Damned fool. A man's as old as he feels. I told him that, but the fellow wouldn't listen.'

He chuckled.

'Would you like to see my home?' the old man asked. He had been watching Anna, noting the look in her eyes, the way she lingered on each feature of the building, admiring the beautifully proportioned windows, the coachhouses and the stables, the meticulously kept yard which once had been busy with the coming and going of a score of hunters and ponies and the whistles of grooms as they worked with their charges. If only the clock could go back; if only changes were for the better and not for worse; if only there was more graciousness now instead of the brash world of redbrick and hideous concrete towers where families were imprisoned in little rooms while boredom reduced the youngsters to hooligans who terrorised their neighbours. If only the kids could live in the country and climb trees and swim in clean rivers and explore and could ride; could find adventure in battling against nature instead of against their neighbours; could release the surge of energy in a place like this.

Anna borrowed a head collar and fastened Tarquin to a ring in the wall, leaving him contemplating, as she followed the old man indoors.

'It's no longer mine,' the old man said. There was only a faint tinge of regret in his voice. 'I'm its custodian. Places like this have no future, except as museums. We can't afford them any more. Everything small and worthwhile is being priced out of existence. Big business will have to take over, and men who work out profitability and know how to make money and keep things going. You'll see it in every walk of life soon; not just mine.'

'I know,' Anna said, her voice bitter. She thought of Compton Hall, now flattened beneath the bulldozers. 'We lived in a place that was a small edition of this. My husband was a farmer. Now it's lying under the new motorway.'

She wasn't used to the idea yet and her voice broke and she had to choke back tears.

The old man led the way through the hall into a room which held a collection of antique silver, protected by glass and burglar alarms; early Georgian cups and bowls and trays gleamed under the lights. There were slender vases and enamelled snuff boxes.

'Things change,' the reedy old voice was gently regretful. 'Once, only a few eyes would have seen these things. Now, they can be shared by many. Hundreds of people come to look at them at the weekends. All kinds of people. Americans, hungry for what they call culture, regretting their own lack of heritage. Women who admire lovely things but can never hope to own them. Everyone can come, providing they pay the entrance fee, which helps to keep them in order for the future generation.'

Anna was herself again. Her eyes relished the line of the more simple jugs and cups and dishes. She did not like ornamentation and hated anything baroque and highly decorated. She chose stark simplicity in her own clothes, avoiding frills and patterns. She stopped to look at a slender vase shaped like a curved leaf, and then moved on.

'Life changes, all the time,' the old man said. 'You have to adapt, or go under. And if you're a fighter, you have to fight; but in the end, you learn to adapt the change to your own ends; you have to, to survive. If I'd gone on fighting this would all have been lost. As it is, I gave it to the nation, and I can end my days in the home in which I was born. You couldn't do that. Your fight was lost before you started. All you can do now is to make a new life; begin again. Don't let them defeat you . . . whoever Them are.'

His dark eyes were laughing at her, but the laughter was kind, and Anna suddenly warmed to him, recognising the soundness of his advice.

'I was over ninety when I made this over to the nation,' he said, leading her back to the hall, having noticed that she was glancing at her watch, anxious about the time. 'Too old to begin again. Too tired. I've had a good life. A long life, and it will be over soon. No one can expect much at ninety-eight, and all I hope is for a quick and graceful ending, not the indignity of a long slow death that bothers everyone about me. I enjoyed my life; enjoy yours, my dear. And good luck.'

He was suddenly tired of her, tired of walking about the room, and he sat down heavily in a chair near the door, looking as fragile as a withered autumn leaf about to be blown from the tree.

Anna went outside and untethered Tarquin, and walked slowly among the trees, savouring the peace. This park had been untouched for centuries. She walked towards the little glade where water sprang over crannied rocks and found herself in a tiny graveyard, of what she thought at first were children's graves. The small grey stones were uniform and she bent to look.

In Memory of Sukie, my little Siamese.
In Memory of Jinty, a black poodle.

A pets' cemetery, where the family pets lay for ever. There could have been no thought of change when this was made. Only of permanency, the family owning the house through the long centuries to come, a symbol of stability. Anna turned her head. The old man was standing in the big doorway, a golden labrador beside him. He lifted his hand and waved. Life went on. It had only been a short encounter, but the old man had comforted her, had given her something of his philosophy. He had lived for almost a century. He had been born long before the motor car era, and the age of television; had seen men land on the moon and dream of visiting the stars; had seen changes beyond imagining when he was young, and had survived them all, bowing to the winds of time but never breaking.

'He's a grand old man. One of the old school,' the gateman said, as Anna led Tarquin back on to the road again.

'Should I have paid to go in?' Anna asked.

'Not into the grounds. And he invited you inside,' the gateman said. 'He can't last long, now, more's the pity. We'll all miss him when he goes. Part of the world here, he is, and a good part. Pity there aren't more like him.'

Anna looked back. The gateman was sweeping the drive again. The house stood firm, long and low and lovely, and above it the wind hurled grey clouds headlong, promising rain.

Anna trotted Tarquin home.

There was purpose in living again.

CHAPTER SIX

Heidi's kid was twenty-five minutes old when Anna reached home. Dan was standing in the shed, looking down, a look of extreme pride on his face. The look was reflected in the goat's face, as she nuzzled her son.

'A lovely little billy goat.' Dan said. 'No trouble at all. Popped out like magic. What shall we call him?'

'Yodel,' Anna said, as the kid bleated suddenly, high and shrill, just discovering his voice. She wanted to pick him up and cuddle him. He was delicious. A promise of a future that held hope. The children would have loved him. She missed the children more each day; even missed Lisetta's untidiness, the clothes she sprawled about her room, the trail of scarves and gloves and boots and coats that always seemed to lie in her wake. No one could ever fail to notice when Lisa had come home.

Philip was tidier, but five times as noisy, erupting into a room explosively, racing up the stairs and down the stairs, slamming the doors when he went out. Yet in spite of his vigour, he was gentle with the animals and had been learning a great deal about farming. He wanted to be a farmer too when he grew up and what future had they to offer him? Perhaps he could be a vet; he would have to work with animals. That was certain.

The kid was already sucking. Every now and then the goat put down her head to lick him, looking at him as if she were afraid he might vanish as mysteriously as he had come. Jezebel was now separated from Heidi. Dan had put a partition in the shed, lest the other goat be jealous. If so, she might attack the kid.

Later that evening, sitting in the dark shed, her head against Jezebel's warm flank, her hands working together rhythmically, squeezing and relaxing, coaxing down the milk, Anna felt serenity restored to herself. Jezebel sensed her new owner's distraction and put her hoof in the bucket. Anna laughed. The kittens could have milk tonight and so could Zelie. Goat's milk would grow fine pups. She locked the shed and went indoors. Dan had cooked sausages and bacon and egg and fried potatoes and was whistling as he laid the table while the Alsatian bitch watched him, lying in the whelping box, her head resting on its side, her eyes interested, as if she were comparing the ways of these new owners to the ones she had left, and finding them extraordinary.

'It's difficult not to credit dogs with human understanding,' Anna said, as the bitch turned to watch her enter the room, and climbed heavily out of the box to come to her new mistress's knee. She was a gentle creature, anxious for reassurance. Anna stroked a smooth head. She was proud of her new acquisition.

'Difficult. But much better not,' Dan said. 'She smells food; that's why she's come. Purest cupboard love.'

'I'm not sure that it is,' Anna said. 'I think she'll whelp tonight. I hope it's easy.'

'No reason why not.' Dan looked out of the window at Suntan who had come close to the glass and was peering inside, hoping that someone would bring him extra rations. He was always hungry, having been half starved for months.

'We can't take one single animal more,' Dan said, as Anna stacked the dishes. 'I don't know how we're going to feed them as it is. Do you realise what it costs?'

Anna nodded. She knew only too well, having that

morning laid in a stock of provender for the goats. It was a good job she had her own savings separate from Dan's money; long years of caring for the little pigs and chickens and her own goats had given her an income, which had rarely been touched.

'Save it for a rainy day,' Dan always said, never imagining that storms lay ahead for them and that Anna's money would prove vital to their future survival. At least she could pay for the goats and the Alsatian; and recoup herself when she sold the pups. With that pedigree they were worth twenty-five pounds each at the very least, and even after deducting the money she had paid the old man, there would surely be a profit. She hadn't yet worked out how much Zelie cost to feed, but fresh meat every day and a pound of cereal, and vitamins, and biscuits, and goat's milk, and eggs all added up. And the pups would need special food when they were weaned. And she couldn't use tins. There wasn't enough nourishment.

'Never count your apples,' Dan said, interpreting her thoughts, and she grinned at him, and then turned all her attention to Zelie, who had retreated to her box and was tramping restlessly around it. An hour later, the first pup was born.

Anna looked at Dan. No trouble there. They went over to Zelie and Anna knelt to praise her, while Dan looked down, remembering all the other younglings he had seen into the world; the calves and the foals and the piglets. A lifetime of birth, each one unique. The raging need for land and farm swept over him suddenly, and he went outside into the darkness to talk to the horses and watch the night close down over Cheshire. There was a glow in the dark, a colouring in the sky above the town, and shreds of cloud drifted round a half moon that held no light. The hum of traffic on the main road on the other side of the big field mocked him, reminding him that soon cars would be speeding over the land that he had nursed and that he had nothing left to pass on to his son. Philip would be bitter when he was old enough to realise his loss. The boy was a born farmer.

There were footsteps in the lane, and Dan walked towards the gate, hoping for conversation. As yet, his neighbours had proved unfriendly but perhaps they were waiting to find out more about the newcomers, not wishing to become involved if they were undesirable. These days, one never knew, and it paid to be wary. They had had odd neighbours of their own in the past; people who borrowed tools and machinery and never returned them; people who imposed on Anna's goodwill; people who seemed to have all day to spare and spent it wasting Anna's time. Dan was less patient with them and would see them off with a sharp sentence, indicating that he was busy. Anna was kinder hearted, though she too would jib when the going was too rough as her patience was not inexhaustible.

Light from the windows flooded the path, revealing the man who stood at the gate, looking at Dan. He had a dog beside him; an incredibly aged collie bitch, walking so slowly that Dan wondered that she was still alive. Her owner was a small man, his face sunken, his eyes half hidden behind thick pebble lenses. He wore an ancient raincoat and a cloth cap.

'You'll be the new people,' he said, as if the statement had been dredged from some subterranean depth after great thought.

Dan nodded.

'Made a lot of changes,' the old man said. 'I remember this in old Billy's day. He lived in the cottage on this side of the garden. Great old poacher, was Billy. Handy with his gun and his family never went short. He had six sons. Lost four of them at Mons, in the war. The other two never did no good. Both died young. Why, young Joe was only seventy-two when he went. No stamina. You wouldn't think I was eighty now, would you?'

Dan shook his head.

'Getting old and so's the old girl, aren't you, Lass?' The collie wagged her tail. 'I used to be shepherd on the farm over there. All houses now. Farmer sold the land and made himself a fortune. I miss the sheep. They say you were a farmer too, mister.'

'I was,' Dan said. 'They've knocked my farm down, to put a motorway across the land. I tried every way I could to fight them but it wasn't any good. We had to go.'

'I dunno what the world's coming to,' the old man said. 'There's trouble enough up here. Men without jobs who've never done anyone a mite of harm; factories closing down because they can't pay the wages the men demand; lads leaving school with never a job to go to; there's as many young ones out of work as old, hereabouts. Ah well, it don't do no good talking about it. Can't alter what's done. Can't change nothing.'

He turned to go, and at the moment Suntan, curious, came trotting across the grass and nuzzled his head against Dan's coat, already affectionate towards the man who had taken him out of the lonely field and who petted him and fed him.

'I heard you'd taken those ponies. Best thing you ever did, mister. None of us could bear to see the way they was kept. These townsfolk who buy ponies for the kids . . . half of them don't know how to keep them. Don't know a thing about horses. I've been feeding them meself when I could cadge a bit of hay, but you can't keep a pony on a pension. Can't keep a dog properly for that matter. But butcher's good and gives us scraps and bones, don't he, Lass?'

The collie wagged her tail and the old man nodded and walked on, his gait as uncertain as that of his dog. He walked to the corner of the fence, and then turned and walked back.

'They tell me in the pet shop you got kittens for sale,' he said.

'Not for sale,' Dan said. 'I'll be glad to get them a good home. Do you want one?'

'Not for meself. For the lass next door. Little lass ten years old; young Susie. She was born blind. They want to get her a dog, but she's scared of them. One jumped at her and knocked her over and not being able to see what did it, she was more frightened than most. She won't even try to make friends with dogs. Maybe a kitten would help.'

'Where do you live?' Dan asked.

'The two cottages at the end of the lane. Down by the school.' The old man pointed. 'Susie's mother's a widow. She was a schoolteacher and she teaches the lass. Bonny little lass, but the mother don't care for dogs much either, so it's tricky. Happen you could help. It's years since there's been animals close. The kid could do with a Guide Dog one day. Be a godsend. Only her mother's against it.'

'I'll see what I can do,' Dan promised. 'Maybe when our two children come home they will help too.'

'You've got children?' the old man asked.

'A girl of sixteen and a boy of twelve,' Dan said. 'They stayed on at their old school, just till the end of the summer term. It's Lisa's O-level year.'

'That's a good school, yonder. It'll do Susie good to have other children here. Her mam's not keen on her playing with just anyone. She's always afraid the lass might get hurt. And she doesn't want her at the Blind school. If Susie went, Dora would have no one left.'

'Would she come with you and call on us?' Dan asked.

'Happen she would,' the old man said. 'She calls me grandad, and she's like me own granddaughters. They live in Australia, so it's good to have Susie close. She's time too, always, to sit and listen, being

61

blind, I suppose. She likes to hear stories about the old days, when I was shepherd on the big farm and there were lambs and sheep to care for, and fields where all them houses are. And this was a pretty little lane, with flowers growing in the hedgerows and you never saw a car down it. I'm always scared Susie might get run over. They go through here so fast.'

He turned away again, and Dan watched him wander into the darkness, a link with the old days, when time moved at a slower pace, and people were friendly and kinder to one another. There had been a shepherd just like him at Compton Hall when Dan was a boy; old Syd, who would never give up in lambing time or take a day off and who took personal responsibility for what he called 'my sheep'. He had known a sight more about sheep than any modern shepherd, and been able to diagnose sheep ills better than any vet. And had some pretty funny cures for them, Dan remembered, as he patted Suntan on the nose and went indoors. Remedies containing honey and herbs and Stockholm tar. And what was more, some of them worked.

There were three puppies in the box beside Zelie. 'She knows exactly what to do, but I think I'll stay with her all the same,' Anna said. 'Go to bed. Then I can sleep in the morning.'

She was nursing Soot who had come to share Zelie's bed, and been put out when the Alsatian growled at him, very softly, warning him away. She was busy and had no time now for kittens. Her real work was starting and she had a job to do. Dan hesitated, wanting to tell Anna about the old man and his dog and about the blind child who was afraid of animals, but this was not the time. Anna had no thought for him. She had already forgotten him and was stroking Zelie and crooning to her, concentrating on the birth.

Dan left her and went up the steep stairs to bed.

He paused on the landing and looked out of the narrow window. Beyond the glass, the sky was broken, stars gleaming between the cloud. The moon had more strength and shone down on the meadow where Tarquin and Sonny merged into a single shadow, leaning against one another for company and warmth. He would build them a shelter. He preferred to have somewhere warm to bed the horses on winter nights, and there was always the fear of coughs and colds and they needed protection then. He had put Suntan and Razzle in the shed with the goats before he came to bed. The ponies were so tiny that there was room for them there, and they had shelter and could not damage the doors with their hooves. It was a very big shed.

The moon gleamed on the water in the corner of the garden, if you could name such a patch of ground a garden. Dan had no time to work on that yet. He would like a pool there; a long, oval pool rimmed with tiny shrubs and flowers; with iris growing in the water and the Muscovies that he had promised Anna. He had always had ducks as part of his life; some of them an absurd part. There had been old Quoddles, who had been caught by a cat when she was only four days old and rescued and nursed in the kitchen, which had become part of her favourite walk ever after, so that she called in on them on her way to the pond, asking for titbits in that weird little chuckling quack that other birds used for their young.

And there had been Misty, who nested in an old barrel, taking straw from the barn to make her bed, tending the bedding fresh every night, leaving a trail of straw behind her, counting heads as the ducklings came off the water, and when all were safe in, she had settled herself in the entrance, with the babies huddled behind her, and had hissed at anyone who looked inside.

He would have to build that pool. He wished it

were bigger as he would like a pair of swans. There was no creature as graceful; they were the epitome of serenity, floating on blue water on a day when the sky was clear. There had been a stream in his grounds, at Compton Hall, and here he had sometimes fished and watched the cob and pen as they guarded their nest.

They would make a new garden, would build a new home from the field and the cottage, would leave a memory behind them. Man needed to build, to leave something permanent to compensate for his own ephemeral existence, to make a mark that others would see. Otherwise, why exist at all? There was no point to living if day succeeded empty day without achievement.

Dan went to bed, and lay awake long into the night, planning his garden, and then, as he drifted into sleep, realised that he, too, was counting apples, and he crossed his fingers and reached out to touch the wooden bedside table and ward off ill luck.

CHAPTER SEVEN

There was no sound at all from downstairs when Dan woke in the morning. He looked at his bedside clock. It was just after six. Old habits die hard. By now he would have been halfway through milking, and for the first time he relaxed, suddenly aware of release from something that, though he had loved it, had been almost a tyranny. The need to get up in the dark, wet or cold, windy or serene, under blue skies and grey skies, in ice and frost and snow, in storm and hail, in sickness as well as in health and bring in the herd and milk each cow, and examine her for any threatened ill.

To clean up and sterilise the equipment, and lug the churns to the end of the lane in time for the milk lorry. Today he had no need. He could lie in bed for another hour if he chose.

He did not choose.

He wanted to be out and to feed the goats; he wanted to see if Zelie had finished pupping. He wanted to give Anna a chance to sleep. He needed to go out and buy wood and build a shed where Zelie could lie with her pups when they were beginning to run about. They couldn't have nine or ten indoors; or even four for that matter, but Alsatians often produced big litters. And it was a good job he had brought one of the big oil heaters with him, as she was a house dog and used to more warmth than a kennel-kept animal, and although the winter had been mild, March could be treacherous and bring frost and snow, and the pups were very small, and small pups always needed warmth.

Dan dressed and went downstairs, and switched on the light. He grinned to himself. Anna was curled on the settee, fast asleep. Three of the kittens were beside her. Smoke had come into the room and was sitting on the arm of the chair near the whelping box, looking down at the pups. She recognised motherhood, and loved small creatures, but she did not go near. Zelie ignored her. She was used to cats. She lay with her body curled. Dan bent to count heads and the bitch licked his hand, welcoming him. He knelt beside her and stroked her shoulders. She made no attempt to repulse him, and he moved her hind leg and put out his finger to count the pups. There were nine, and she was not unduly protective, which would save trouble. A bitch that guarded too fiercely was a very noisy companion.

There was a small movement beyond Zelie.

Another pup, lying at her back, Dan thought, and went to shift it. It was Soot, who had adopted Zelie for his own mother and found her warmer and more companionable than Smoke, who was becoming tired of a maternal role and tended now to walk away from her offspring. Soot opened his mouth in a wide pink yawn and Dan laughed, amused by the kitten. Soot yowled and stretched. Now Dan was up there would be food in the kitchen, and he was a greedy mite, liable to push his brothers and sisters away from their plates and take their share.

Anna was awake.

She stretched herself too, and yawned. She was stiff and uncomfortable and wanted a bath.

'She finished whelping about four o'clock,' Anna said, coming to look down at the litter and stroke Zelie and praise her. 'No trouble at all. She knows exactly how to cope. They're lovely pups. Very lively.'

It was amazing how such young creatures could seem so strong, Dan thought. They were moving against one another, blind heads turning to nuzzle, pushing with their paws as they fed, squeaking surprisingly noisily. Soot walked over and sniffed them, mystified. Zelie growled softly. She didn't mind him at her back, but he wasn't coming in among her babies. Soot walked away, his tail an irate exclamation mark.

'I cleaned out the paper and gave her fresh bedding,' Anna said, pushing her hair out of her eyes and yawning again. 'You'll have to burn it. Make coffee while I bath, Dan.'

The bath was bliss. Lying in hot water, looking at the tiled walls that had replaced the old yellow distemper, Anna relaxed. The pups were strong and healthy, their breeding was splendid, and it was the gateway to a new mode of life. She would keep Zelie and the best bitch puppy and at least one of the dogs; perhaps two, and found her own kennels. She could breed from Zelie again; and in two years' time she'd have a second bitch to breed from. She could sell six of the pups at at least thirty pounds each; one hundred and eighty pounds would surely give her some profit towards keeping four dogs. She had never worked out the cost of feeding an Alsatian.

The birth had been easy; Zelie was not unduly exhausted. Anna had given her a drink of milk and glucose and seen that all the pups had had a feed. Life was on the upsurge again. Maybe it was going to be hard; they would always be short of money. The two cottages had cost a fortune, and only ten years ago the landlord was probably hard put to it to find a tenant, let alone a buyer. One of the cottages in the lane two miles away from Compton Hall had been bought for four thousand pounds five years before the motorway was mooted, in the expectation that the road would pass over the land. But the route was changed. This did not stop the buyer from making a handsome profit as he sold the place for over seventeen thousand pounds to a stockbroker wanting a country retreat that was close to the main route. The whole area would change now, Anna thought sadly, watching the sun slant across the ceiling. If only progress could be halted and some of the old things left. Not all were bad.

She was almost asleep. She dressed herself hurriedly and went downstairs to find that Dan had breakfasted and gone outside. She poured herself some coffee and cut bread to put in the toaster, and watched Smoke settle herself in the sunshine and hold down one of the kittens and wash it. She must find them homes. It was ridiculous to have seven cats. She'd keep Soot who had enchanted her, and have him neutered. The others must go. One was already spoken for. She hoped the old man would bring the blind child to see her. Dan had told her about the child before she bathed. It would make a welcome break in the loneliness. She and Dan were too much in one another's pockets, with no one to call. If only striking new roots was easier, but how did you do it? Anna did not know. She was unwilling to use the church to ease herself into her new home, as that often meant responsibility in one way or another, and there was never time if there were animals to care for.

Dan came inside a few minutes later, a frown on his face. It was a familiar look, and Anna's mood changed at once. It was a look that meant trouble. It also meant that Dan's temper would be unpredictable and she would have to watch her tongue. Better to say nothing until he chose to enlighten her. He went out again almost at once, shutting the door forcefully behind him. No good trying to find out what was wrong. That would provoke a stormy attack on Anna herself. She always bore the brunt of the family's worries.

Zelie needed feeding. No meat for the first day. Anna mixed up goat's milk and a beaten egg and put it beside the whelping box. Zelie was a delightful mother. Anna had not needed to help. She had sat watching, ready to assist if anything went wrong, knowing from the bitch's twisting and turning and panting and groaning that birth was soon to begin. As soon as the first pup was born, Zelie settled, lifting it gently from the ground beneath her tail and laying it firmly against her crossed front paws, on its back, while she bit the cord and cleaned away the birth membranes. When she was satisfied that the pup was as clean as her tongue could make it, she tucked it against her. By then a second was born, and the procedure was repeated. The whole litter came within five hours.

Twice during the morning Anna looked out of the window, but Dan was in the goat shed and had not reappeared when the old man came up the garden path, a slender child beside him. Anna saw a fair-haired girl with wide blue eyes that did not reveal the fact that she was blind. She held the old man's arm and walked confidently. She was a beautiful child, slightly made, her cheekbones high and elegant.

Anna went to the kitchen door.

'This is Susie,' the old man said. 'And I'm Len Farrow. I didn't tell your man, did I, Missus? I hope it's all right to call now. We could come back later.'

'Come in,' Anna said, glad of distraction. Dan came running out of the shed and drove off in the car without saying a word. 'I don't want to disturb Zelie and her puppies now, but Susan can hold one of the kittens. Perhaps you'd like one to take home?'

'Mummie says I can have a kitten,' Susan said. 'Tell me about them. And please . . .' she hesitated, and Len spoke for her.

'She wants to "see" you with her hands,' he said. 'Then she'll know what you look like.'

Anna knelt and took the child's hands and put them to her face.

'You're small,' Susan said at once. 'Nearly as small as me. And your hair's long.'

'I haven't done it yet,' Anna said. 'I sat up all night with Zelie, and I was too lazy this morning. I'm going to have a rest this afternoon, as no one ever calls.'

'What colour are your eyes?' Susan asked.

'Grey-green,' Len said, looking at Anna. 'And her skin's brown with the sun, and her hair's brown too.'

'Nice colours,' Susan said. Her hands lingered on the fabric of Anna's blouse. 'It's soft and silky. I like its feel.'

She put her hand out against the kitchen wall.

'Paint,' she said at once. 'Is the room big?'

'Smaller than your kitchen at home. Not as small as mine,' Len said.

'Do you know colours?' Anna asked, curious, wondering if the child had ever been able to see at all, and could remember.

'In a sort of way,' Susan said. 'There's yellow, like the sun; it's a hot colour, a nice colour. The colour

69

of daffodils and cowslips; a growing colour. And there's grey, like dead ashes in the fireplace and cold days with rain on my face; and there's blue like the sky on a hot day and warm water and Len's budgerigar that's little and soft and nibbles my fingers and sings to me. And there's brown, like Mummie's hair and eyes; her hair's soft too, and curly. I can twist the curls round my fingers. And there's white; that's a cold colour, like our refrigerator, and the washing machine and the cooker. And there's red, that's warm, like woodfires.'

'Come into the sitting-room,' Anna said. 'Would you like some coffee?'

'Can I have milk, please?' Susan asked. Len had led her across to the settee, and at once her small hands slid over the arms, feeling the shape, feeling the texture of the fabric, all her life in her fingers.

Soot was on the windowsill, watching birds. He came to see the visitors, and Len took the child's hand and put it on the kitten's soft fur.

'He's black,' Len said.

'He's warm, and he's purring.' Susan was delighted. The kitten rubbed against her arm. She put her hands around him. 'He's so small, and such little bones. What are his eyes like?'

'Green, like the grass,' Len said. Anna could hear them talking as she made the coffee and poured the milk. The old man had learned to adapt himself to Susan and to make up to her for some of the lack in her life, but she was a happy child, with a ready delighted smile and an appreciation of anything that was said to her.

'Shall I tell you about Zelie?' Anna asked when she had handed out coffee cups and given the child a glass of milk, and Susan had felt the outline and nodded her head.

'It's like Len's glasses,' she said. 'Curvy. Mummie's are straight and there are pictures on them. I can feel them with my fingers. Please tell me about Zelie.'

'She's an Alsatian,' Anna said. 'A very big dog, and she's very gentle. She likes to lie by my legs with her head on my feet and have her ears stroked. And she has nine puppies. The puppies Len told you about, or didn't he?'

Susan nodded.

'Grandad said you might let me have one,' she said, and Anna agreed quickly and realised she had already knocked thirty pounds off her profit as she couldn't possibly charge the child's mother that amount. 'If I like it. Dogs are so rough,' Susan added.

'Will your mother let you have it at home?' Anna asked.

Susan shook her head.

'She doesn't like dogs much and she doesn't like Alsatians at all. Grandad said he thought you could keep it here for me, and I could come and play with it. And then maybe Mummie would come too and see how nice it was and I can have a proper Guide Dog to take me out when Grandad and Mummie are busy. I can't go near any roads alone.'

There was the sound of the car returning. Zelie had left her pups and gone into the garden. She barked, and then recognised Dan's voice, and greeted him, her tail waving. The Alsatian came back into the room, and Dan followed her, not expecting visitors. He was about to speak when he saw them, and nodded to Len and the child, forgetting she was blind.

'Who is it?' Susan asked.

'Only my husband,' Anna said. 'He's been shopping and just come home and Zelie's with him. Would you like to stroke her before she goes back to her puppies?'

Susan shook her head and looked towards Dan.

'You feel like Mummie does when she's worried,' she said, and Dan looked at the child, startled.

'Susan can't see, but she's a great one for knowing how people feel,' Len said, realising that Dan had forgotten that the child could not see at all.

'I am worried,' Dan said. 'Anna, the goat's ill and we'll have to have the vet. Have you got his phone number?'

'I can do better than that,' Len said. 'I've got to go there myself to pick up some pills for Lass. She has a bad heart. I'll tell him what you want, just as soon as I've taken Susie home.'

'Would you like to take the kitten with you?' Anna asked.

'I can drive you back,' Dan said.

'Please,' Susan said. 'The black one?'

'Not the black one,' Anna said. 'I want to keep him.' She avoided Dan's eyes. 'There's a dear little grey one. I'll find him for you. He's just like his mother.'

The grey kitten was lying on the landing in a brief patch of sunshine. He nestled into Anna's arms as she lifted him, and went straight to Susan, cuddling against her neck, purring loudly, loving the feel of human hands about him.

'Can I drive you on to the vet?' Dan asked.

'That would be a rare help,' the old man said. 'It's a tidy step and my legs aren't as young as they were. Come on, Susie. Mind the step, lovie. Hold on tight.'

Dan turned his head to look at Anna and for a moment their eyes met. She knew that he felt as she did, pitying the child and yet, oddly, the child neither needed nor asked for pity. She was self-reliant and happy, leading an inner life that seemed to make up for everything she missed, and she had a vivid sense of words for a child of ten. It must have come from a life among older people and time spent thinking instead of seeing.

'Is the goat bad?' Anna asked softly, before Dan went out.

'I think she's going to die,' Dan said bleakly. 'And

that will leave us with an orphan to rear; I don't think the other goat will accept the kid.'

Life never went smoothly for more than ten seconds, Anna thought forlornly as Dan went out. Never count apples . . .

She went indoors, to find that Zelie had evicted Soot from her box. The kitten was standing facing the bitch with her fur ruffled, swearing at her, while Smoke flew in to defend him. She fielded Smoke and evicted both cats and went into the kitchen to make up more food for the Alsatian.

There was a crash from outside. Razzle had knocked the dustbin over and was nosing among the rubbish. Anna went out to shift him and clear up the mess, and wondered what on earth had possessed her to get landed with more animals when she might have had a rest.

The pony nuzzled her affectionately. His small head was hard against her arm, and she noticed again how attractive he was with shaggy mane and tail and thick winter coat and the glowing brown eyes that welcomed anyone who had time to talk to him. He would soon be very handsome indeed. So would Suntan. She crossed her fingers. She would soon be as superstitious as Dan. Touch wood and don't reckon on a good harvest. Hope for the best but don't bank on it. She would have her rest and then write to the old man who had owned Zelie and tell him about the puppies, and one day soon she would drive over and tell him that his animals were all well.

He must miss Zelie horribly. Life was never fair.

CHAPTER EIGHT

It was no good. Jezebel refused to feed Heidi's kid under any circumstances at all. She kicked and she butted and she twisted away. The kid was terrified, and Anna ended by taking him indoors, into the warm kitchen, where he stood watching her prepare a feeding bottle, filled with Jezebel's warmed milk. He took it without fuss, sucking greedily, and Anna realised that he could have had very little milk from his own mother.

Heidi was lying in the straw, taking no interest in the world at all. Suppose she had to tell the old man that one of his beloved goats was already dead and that she was having to hand-rear the kid. Surely they couldn't be so unlucky? She found an enormous cardboard grocery box in the garage outside, lined it with newspaper, and tucked the kid inside. He would sleep now he had been fed, but he was little and agile and would be very mischievous and she couldn't keep him indoors. No use putting him back with his mother, and Jezebel wouldn't tolerate him.

Dan and the vet arrived simultaneously. Scott Lewis was a tall man, his thick fair hair already greying, and Anna realised as he walked towards the shed that he was much older than he looked. He saw her at the window and nodded, his mind preoccupied. Anna longed to go and find out what he thought was wrong, but made herself wait. Meantime, now he was here, perhaps he could look at Zelie and the pups and make sure that nothing went wrong there.

It seemed ages before the two men came indoors. Anna had made coffee. It had been a routine with their vet at Compton Hall, and they would need to know this one too, since they were obviously going to have more animals than she had imagined in their new home.

'It's just a fever,' Dan said. 'She's got a high temperature but nothing else seems to be wrong.'

'There's no second kid, I think it's just an infection,' the vet said, taking his coffee gratefully. He was not going to have time for lunch. 'And there's no sign of any other trouble. She should take a turn for the better tonight, if she is going to recover, but she's pretty sick. I've given her an injection. And I'd better see her in the morning.'

He looked down at the kid.

'You'll have your hands full with that,' he commented. 'But old Jenkinson put his beasts in good hands. He was lucky. I was rather worried about them. The people round here aren't animal trained at all. It's mainly a dormitory area, where even the women seem to commute and there's no one at home all day.'

'I never thought that losing our own home would mean we could do good elsewhere,' Dan commented. 'The bitch has whelped too. I suppose you know her as well as the goats.'

'Not all that well,' Scott said, putting his cup down on the draining board. 'She's only been to me for her inoculations and the booster, and a cut on her paw from glass. She's a healthy little thing.'

'Not so little when she's indoors,' Anna commented, leading the way into the big living-room. The whelping box was next to the big radiator, to keep the pups warm. Little pups were vulnerable to chilling and as they never shivered, there was no way of getting them warm if they got cold.

Scott looked down at the litter, and smiled. Soot had come back and was curled against Zelie's back, his expression blissful. He was warm and very comfortable. Smoke was asleep on the windowsill, lying

75

in a patch of sunlight, and the other four kittens were curled together in a heap on the settee, lying on Anna's cardigan which she had thrown down some minutes before.

'Do you want homes for them?' Scott asked.

Anna nodded.

"All except Soot. He's the one in Zelie's box. Do you know of anyone who wants a kitten? We gave one to the little blind girl. It will need inoculating.'

'Len will see to that,' Scott said. 'And if you ever need a nurse for your animals, call him in. He's splendid with them. He must have been a first-class shepherd. And you should see the dogs he trains. He used to win all the cups at the sheepdog trials and he can still teach a collie better than most men. He's a character, is old Len. I want a kitten myself. I've got to put our old cat down soon, as he's going on sixteen and showing his age. It will help if we have his replacement beforehand. My small daughter can't bear to lose any pet.'

He bent to look more carefully at Zelie, who accepted him quietly. She watched anxiously as he lifted each pup and examined it, but made no protest, only licking it all over when he put it down again.

'That's a very healthy-looking litter,' Scott said, as he stood up and dusted the knees of his trousers. He bulked large in a thick fleece-lined short coat, and wore a dark suit with a blue flowered shirt and matching tie. Nothing like Jack Hoskins, their old vet at Compton Hall who invariably wore an ancient roll-neck jersey and grey flannels that never saw an iron, and who stripped off to his underpants to deliver a calf and then stood under the pump to wash himself down. Tough as a man could be, Jack had been.

Scott chose the second grey kitten and tucked it under his coat where it lay quiet, used to being handled. All the kittens came each evening to be nursed, loving to sit on Dan or Anna, and trusting them completely. Anna glanced at the calendar as she took Scott to the door. They had already lived here for more than a month and so much had happened that it seemed impossible to realise that only a few weeks ago she had been desolate. If only the goat survived. Anna could not bear any creature in her care to die. They should have watched more closely. Surely they would have seen signs of trouble?

There was a crash from the kitchen.

Anna ran outside. The kid was awake and had jumped from his box on to the kitchen table, sending two cups on to the floor, where they had shattered. What on earth could she do with him? She took him up to the empty bedroom, which was awaiting new furniture, as she was giving Lisetta a bedsitter where she could take her friends. The little animal could do no damage in a bare room, and perhaps by tonight he could go back to his mother. Meanwhile she had better milk Jezebel again and make sure he was provided with enough food for the day.

She went into the goat shed. Heidi was lying quietly and lifted her head as Anna came in. She seemed better already. Perhaps the infection would go down quickly. They had called the vet in at once. The nanny had shown no sign of trouble the night before.

She glanced up as a shadow darkened the doorway.

'Came to see if there was anything I could do,' Len said, looking down at the goat. 'Looks as if you got that in time. She'll perk up fast now she's had a bit of treatment. Wonderful how well animals recover.'

Anna had been about to say there was nothing that needed doing when she looked up and saw the wistful expression in the old man's eyes.

'Can you finish milking while I get Zelie's food ready?' she asked, and Len grinned at her as if she had given him the highest honour she could think of.

'I miss the beasts,' he said. 'And farmer over yonder's not the sort to want telling. He don't have no time for anyone, that one. So no use calling. I come down to help your husband with the new kennel, but he's not got the wood yet.'

'He was going to buy it this morning,' Anna said.

'I know a fellow as 'as got a load of good wood going cheap. It's part of a house that's been demolished. Painted, too, so it won't need much attention. There's not enough for the whelping kennel, but it'd do fine to make partitions in the big kennel block.'

'What big kennel block?' Anna asked blankly.

'I reckon I'm talking out of turn,' Len said. He grinned up at Anna, a gap-toothed grin that split his wrinkled face. His eyes shone behind the thick glasses. 'You old man were telling me on the way to the vet that you might start breeding for pleasure, like, and he thought it a good idea. I said as there weren't any decent boarding kennels anywhere near here and if he had room and could take a few dogs in he'd be earning money for himself and doing some good too. So, as there's room down the end there for a big kennel block, we went and bought an old hut and it's coming tomorrow.'

'Some people,' Anna said, and laughed. 'He didn't say a word about it to me. And since I know who'll be likely to feed the dogs and clean the kennels, he might have asked me.'

'Maybe he wanted to surprise you,' Len said. His quick fingers were busy and Jezebel stood stockstill, her milk pouring down into the pail. 'Like old times,' the old man went on, as he leaned his head against her. 'I used to have two nannies when Mother was alive. She liked goats' milk, and goats' cheese. Been dead near on ten years, and I still miss her, though we argued like pernickety bantam cocks all our days. Pity you can't go together. There's always one left. Did I tell yer that Mrs. Jenkinson died in 'ospital yesterday night, so the old boy's on his own?'

78

'Will he want Zelie back?' Anna asked.

'I doubt it, Missus. She needs a lot of looking after and he's not one to put himself first. He'll be glad you've got her. He knows he couldn't manage alone.'

And he'll be lonely, Anna thought as she went indoors. Life was cruel to the old. Leaving them desolate when they were least able to cope. She had never even seen the old lady, but she was sad to think that Mrs. Jenkinson would never know that the bitch had a fine healthy litter. As soon as she could get away for a short while she would drive over and tell the old man. He would surely want to know. She could write, but she had no idea what to say.

She went inside again to feed Zelie, making up another meal of milk and beaten egg and glucose for the bitch, taking care not to overload her immediately after whelping. Zelie herself was very busy, tucking the pups down close against her, nosing them into position, watching them feed and then licking each one to clean it up afterwards. Her box was immaculate.

'Lucky for some, unlucky for others,' Len said, coming in a moment later with the bucket full of milk. 'You can't live without animals, no more than me. I've always got a shed full of injured birds. The kids bring them to me. Old Len'll make it better, they say, and often I can. Got a sparrow there now that a cat brought in. It's got a broken wing, but it's mending and he's that cheeky he'll perch on my hand to eat. Well, I'd best be getting along. My old Lass'll be missing me, and it's time she had a walk.'

He nodded and went out, and Anna watched him plod slowly down the path and stop to pat Razzle who trotted towards the old man, hoping to find pony nuts in his pocket. Len grinned, and found a sugar lump and handed it over. He always had titbits for animals, and all the horses in the fields nearby knew him well.

Lucky for some, unlucky for others, Anna

79

repeated the words to herself as she worked that day. Funny how life could change and change so completely that when you looked back you wondered how it had been possible. And yet, if you paused to consider, you could see the pointers, one after another, leading inevitably to a new beginning. If one door closed another opened. Dan's father had also always said that. He was a great one for proverbs and many of those he used he invented, Anna was certain.

He had been a wonderful man and she still missed him. And she missed her own grandfather. He could do anything with animals, could bring them back from the gateway of death itself, his old cowman had said. And old Jed the cowman had been a character too. They didn't come like that any more.

Anna went out to look at Heidi. The goat was sleeping. If only she recovered.

If only.

The story of human existence in two absurd words.

But there was work to do and no time for brooding, and Smoke was asking for food, and so were the kittens. Soot brushed against her leg, vociferous. It was well past feeding time. She had forgotten all about the cats and, as she opened the tins and spooned the mixture on to the plates, Soot forgot his manners and, in his impatience, bit her leg.

CHAPTER NINE

Life never stood still. Heidi recovered. The days sped by so fast that Anna wondered how it had happened. Len and Dan worked on the new kennel. Two weeks passed and Zelie was able to go, with her pups, into a big shed with an outside run. Dan had built a corner box indoors where she could lie and feed her babies, and a friend of Len's, a taciturn little man called Sid, had fitted up an infra red lamp so that Dan did not need the clumsy oil stove. Anna hated the stove. It smelled and she was always afraid of fire.

Two more weeks. The middle of March and the days had warmed sufficiently for the pups, now over a month old, to come out into the run and play together, nine sturdy little roly poly bundles of fluffy fur. They were strongly marked, black and gold, with delightful faces and floppy ears, already showing their characters. They were bold little creatures and enjoyed watching the cars that sped down the lane. They could see through the front gate, an affair of iron bars that Dan had covered with thick wire mesh to keep the animals from escaping.

Susan often came with Len and spent her time listening to Anna talking as she worked. The blind child loved cuddling the cats and, after some persuasion, consented to have one pup at a time indoors to play with too. She was soon enraptured. It was good for puppy as well as child. Susie learned to pull a twist of thick rope and wriggle it for the puppy to pounce and tug. She began to delight in the feel of the tugging animal, and Anna loved to hear the child laugh as the puppy began to tease and growl.

Susie also loved to go out and stroke the goats and was beginning to allow the ponies to come to her and to stroke their noses. Anna took care to see that none of the animals could push or butt, and held them by a halter or a leading rein on one side of the gate, while Susan stood on the other. Soon they recognised the little blind girl's voice when she called to them and answered her with shrill whinnies that delighted her.

The house was no longer empty. Len and Sid often dropped by to collect Dan and go off for a jar at the pub. The vet was a constant visitor too, coming in once or twice a week to join the men, and he had earmarked one of Zelie's puppies for himself. He came by on the day that the pups were eight weeks old and found Anna standing miserably in the kitchen, holding a letter and a cheque.

'Trouble?' Scott asked, quick to sense that she was distressed. Dan and Len were busy at the far end of the garden, putting up the big kennels.

'Old Mr Jenkinson's dead too,' she said. 'He never cashed the cheque I gave him for Zelie and the goats. His son's sent it back, saying he's only too glad I have them and that they are being taken good care of. And do I know anyone who wants the two cats.'

'Two old cats,' Scott said. 'Black and Tan. He's had them for about eight years. They won't settle with anyone else. But they might settle with Zelie.'

Two more cats. But she couldn't let them live wild, or be put down, so that when Scott brought the pair of them over that night, she took them into the living-room and let Zelie join them there. Both cats knew the Alsatian well. Zelie was now sleeping in the house again while the pups crowded in the whelping box, in a close packed mass. Anna left the two cats; they curled up at once on the floor, close to Zelie, and seemed to know that they now had a new home. Their master had been dead for four days. They had been lonely in the deserted cottage. He had always made much of them.

'It was his heart too,' Len said, coming to the kitchen for coffee. 'He were nearly ninety and it just gave out. Missed his old lady. Died quiet in his chair and next door found him when he went in to see why the old boy hadn't been along to collect his paper from the end of the lane. They leave it in a drainpipe there, and all the post. Proper country, not like here, though it were like that here in my young days. By the way, there's a lady over the other side of Chadleigh wants a pup. Her old Alsatian's had to go. Fifteen and such bad arthritis it couldn't walk properly. She'll know how to look after one of yours but you need to be careful who you let have 'em. There's a young couple had three dogs in two years. Two got run over and the last one was put down because they wanted to go to Spain for their 'olidays and they want one of the pups. Name's Smith. I'll tell yer when they come, and don't you sell one to them, whatever you do. Those are good pups.'

They were good pups. Anna looked at them daily when she fed them. They were now weaned and separated from Zelie, who had come into the house again and settled in her old corner. Zelie followed Anna round as she worked, knowing that Anna was her main charge and the pups were a necessary and infrequent intrusion in her life.

There were three that were especially good. Anna had been studying Alsatians diligently, reading books about the breed, noting the points and looking closely at photographs of the leading champions. She wanted a brood bitch and she wanted at least one stud dog. She would keep two of the dogs and pretend that one belonged to Susan. She had met the child's mother and it was very plain that the pup would never be allowed to go to the blind girl's home. The mother disliked animals and felt that they had no place in the modern world. She was not an easy woman to talk to and Anna wondered if Susan's mother resented her daughter having any life of her own and wanted to keep her dependent. But Susan was strong minded and the mother had little success if that was her aim.

'Can I name the pups?' Susan asked.

It was the first litter Anna had ever had. The litter letter would be A. The pups required registering and she hadn't got a Kennel prefix. She would need that too and it wasn't easy to choose a new and distinctive name.

' "A" names?' Susan said. She was holding the little bitch that Anna had determined to keep, a strong minded and wilful little animal with a delightful extrovert temperament and a merry little face. Her eyes sparkled up at Anna and her ears were already beginning to prick. One dropped back to the side of her head, and she sat, lop eared, roly poly, and Susan hugged her suddenly.

'Arachne,' Susan said.

'I'm not sure I want a puppy named after a spider,' said Anna, laughing. 'What about Astronaut for your little dog? Astro for short.'

'Astro . . . that's a nice name. And Argonaut for yours. Argon. And that just leaves the little girl dog. Acacia.'

'Not Acacia,' Anna said. She was never going to be able to think up nine names beginning with A and register the litter.

'Alabaster,' said Susan.

'That would do for one of the other little dogs. It doesen't sound very feminine.'

Anna was turning over the pages of the dictionary.

'What about Ambrosia?' she asked. 'Amba for short.'

'What does that mean?' Susan had rolled the puppy on to his back and was fingering the fur round his ears. She had completely lost all fear; she had handled them daily and their growth had been so gradual that she had not noticed the change.

'It's a drink for Immortals in the old legends,' Anna said. 'It sounds pretty. We'll call ours Amba, Argon and Astro. And we must think up some more names for the rest, and a kennel prefix for all my dogs, so that people recognise them.'

'Annally,' said Susan. 'That's how it sounds if you say Anna Leigh very quickly. Annally Astro and Annally Argon and Annally Amba.'

It was a good idea and Anna adopted it, unable to

think of anything better. Easter was very late that year and the pups would all be sold before the children came home, except for the three she was running on. They would become part of their home, along with four cats and four horses, and the two goats as Heidi had now recovered. Anna intended to sell the kid. He was an imp of mischief and his favourite diet appeared to be tablecloths which he ate whenever she pegged one up on the line, if he was free to get at it.

The end of March and Len and Dan had completed fencing the garden and field. They had put in jackal fencing, which was high wire with concrete posts that sloped inwards at intervals. This meant the pups could run free without fear of escape and Anna was able to release them for a riot. They raced in a pack, turning and chasing and rolling over one another, and she loved watching them. Soon passers-by in the lane stopped to watch, and before very long she had buyers for all six pups, more buyers than she needed so that she was able to ask what sort of home the pup would go to and ensure that no one with a tiny house bought a dog that would occupy far more space than was available. She also made discreet inquiries as to whether the prospective owners realised how much food a grown dog needed, and if they had any reservations about grown Alsatians as many people suffered from the misconception that the animals were vicious.

By the end of the first week in April all were sold. Anna missed the puppies but was delighted with the three they had kept. Each was different. Argon was a quiet dog, his ears quickly coming erect, his manners beautiful. His only fault was a rather narrow head, but that would remedy with time. Amba was the boss of the litter, chasing her brothers away from their plates so ruthlessly that they had to be fed separately. Anna could not decide which one she liked best. Astro was the clown of the three, and she

thought he would make the best dog. He was beautifully built, with good bone and a strong body. His
head was broad and doggy, his brown eyes were
wide, placid and very alert, but his ears tumbled in a
flop on either side of his head and refused to stay up,
giving him a benign expression that was all his own.

He was affectionate and excitable, first to come
when Anna brought food or opened the kennel, ready
to exclaim in an ear-piercing squeak at anything that
happened to him, standing up on hind legs at the
wire to watch what went on around him.

It was an excellent site for the whelping kennel
as all the pups could see the world around them.
Traffic sped down the lane; boys on bicycles; large
lorries taking a short-cut through to the main road at
the far end; all the rush-hour cars, saving themsleves
a mile and a half in distance and two sets of traffic
lights. The passers-by on foot were fewer, but many
stopped to admire the pups, and now the children
who paused at the gate spoke to Anna, and to Susan
if she were there.

One morning a small man knocked at the back
door. He was no taller than Anna, chunkily built with
a thick mass of untidy grey-blond hair.

'Nice pups you've got there,' he commented.

'They're not for sale,' Anna said, suspicious, and
was startled when the man handed her a visiting
card.

Mike Redwood. Alsatian Handler.

'I handle in the ring for a number of people round
here,' he said. 'Scott Lewis told me about your three
pups. He thinks they have a great future. So do I. I
specially like the fellow with the floppy ears. If those
stand up soon, you've got a real winner on your
hands. I know Zelie. I used to show her for poor old
Jim Jenkinson when his son went away. He got forty
quid each for her first pups. What did you sell them
for?'

'Between twenty and thirty, depending,' Anna

said. She had let two go cheap to people whose old dogs had died and who had turned away sadly when they heard the price. She knew just how they felt and couldn't bear to think of them returning to a house without a dog in it.

'You can't let your heart rule your head in this game,' Mike said

'I'm breeding because I want to; and I'll do it my own way,' Anna said, resenting advice from a complete stranger.

Mike grinned at her, in no way abashed.

'You do it your way then,' he said. 'You'll be out of pocket. If you ever want a handler, let me know. I'd like to show those three. They're super little pups.'

The big run of kennels was finished and Anna moved the pups. Amba and Argon were fighting Astro, making his life a misery. They were better separated. Dan was drafting an advertisement, and Scott had already found them two boarders for August and more would come. Most owners had to drive thirty miles to find a reliable kennel. Dan had applied for a licence and no one could fault the accommodation.

Two days after Mike Redwood had called, Scott arrived with an Alsatian bitch in his car.

'Could you board her until she whelps and sell the pups afterwards?' he asked. 'She's one of my patients. I promised I'd try.' He grinned at Anna, knowing she would not have the heart to refuse. 'Her owner's had to go into hospital for a major operation and won't be able to cope with the bitch at all. She is as gentle as Zelie. The pups are well bred. I'll bring you the pedigrees of bitch and sire if you'll take them. And if there is a little bitch there that looks good, you might like her. They come from the same breeder as Zelie, but from different parents. Her owner would like you to sell the pups and hopes that will cover the boarding costs.'

Their first boarder was going to be more of a tie

than Anna had expected, but the thought of more puppies was fun, and her own three could now be moved into the big kennel run. The bitch, a pretty animal with more gold than black in her fur, named Zinta, was heavily in whelp. Anna just turned in time as Zelie growled, preparing to attack the intruder.

'Zelie, NO,' Anna shouted, and Zelie stopped at once, but remained with ruff raised and eyes glaring, while Scott hastily took the newcomer outside the gate and Anna took her own Alsatian into the house. Zelie would need to be watched. She regarded the property as hers, and now protected Anna assiduously, warning off all strangers.

Anna shut Zelie in the house. She put Zinta in the end kennel in the big run. She wanted to scrub and disinfect the whelping kennel before the bitch went inside. And Dan had just let the musketeers out for exercise. The pups raced round the grass and vanished, heading for the pond, which Dan had still not managed to dredge and put in order. Anna went to collect them and bring them in. It was still too chilly for swimming.

They had not gone into the water. They had found an old rag lying by the edge of the pond and were busy pulling and tugging trying to get it away from one another. Amba ran off, her small face impish with enjoyment, and she shook it vigorously, sending mud all over Anna who made a grab at the rag and failed to get it.

Argon ran in and snatched it, and two seconds later Astro had hold of it and was charging down the field, with the two other pups in pursuit. Dan, coming across from the kennel block, stepped in and grabbed the cloth, and wrinkled his nose in disgust at its stink.

The pups stank too when Anna shut them separately in the big kennesl. She took Amba in first. The little bitch was liable to be obstreperous and fight both her brothers, unless someone was there to stop them. Anna was not at all sure that the two dogs, kennelled together, would not fight too. And at this stage a fight could be for real and would be serious. She remembered her old Collie Meg who had met a little sister for the first time after eight years and had gone for her. Meg had sixteen stitches and the other bitch had twenty-five, and they had never been able to stand the sight of one another afterwards. Anna had offered to look after Meg's sister while her owner went on holiday. It had been a terrible three weeks, as both bitches had to be separated all the time and Meg had barked like a lunatic every time the visitor was exercised. Luckily the bites had healed cleanly and by the time the owners came home the stitches were out and there was little to show for the attack, but for several days Anna had feared she would have a dead dog to own up to when her friends returned. Never again would she offer to look after another dog without proper accommodation for it, she had vowed then.

One thing, she would remember, and that was one mistake less to make now they were starting up in business.

That night Setter's Dene took on a new aspect, with a second bitch in the whelping kennel, the three pups in the big block, and Zelie in the house, lying at Anna's feet. Anna sat down to watch television briefly before going to bed, aware that all her charges were fed and safe and that soon she could start thinking about entering her pups for their first show. She was positive that Astro would be the founder of a great line of Alsatians. He was growing more splendid every day, and Scott had commented, only that morning, that she could pride herself on Zelie's progeny and before long would find she had begun to make a name in the Show ring with them.

Her Three Musketeers. They were already ten weeks old. They were gay little dogs and she was far too fond of them, especially of Argon; or was it Astro who was her favourite? Or wicked little Amba, who had stolen Dan's shoes and left one in the muck heap and the other in the pond, and had taken the yard broom and chewed off all the bristles, and who had treed all the cats at once and sat beneath them, her tongue hanging out and her face mischievously alive with excitement.

It was Amba who found Anna's glove lying on the path and took it to the pond. Anna found it there two days later, ruined beyond wearing. Yet the little bitch was quick to learn, and when Anna had had them inoculated, and began to walk them, it was Amba who was the easiest to teach to sit, though Argon was the pup that never needed to be taught to keep to heel.

Astro was impossible at first. Walking excited him so much that he progressed in leaps, jumping up at Anna, exclaiming at everyone and everything that passed them. If he saw a bird in the hedge, Astro squealed; if he saw a cat cross the lane, he had to comment; and when he had commented he had to be told he was a good dog, had to bound at Anna, or cling to her legs with crossed paws, desperate for affection. He was the funniest little pup she had ever handled.

Mike Redwood had taken to calling in daily, watching their progress with an informed eye. Anna discovered that he had handled Alsatians for over thirty years, and drove all over the country to show them for breeders. She soon discovered his name was widely known and that he had a small but thriving business selling leads and collars and obedience dumb-bells, and petfood at wholesale prices. Anything she wanted for the animals, Mike found. He brought her a batch of enamel feeding and drinking bowls one day, which cost half the price of those in the shops, and another day he came with the offer of a hatch of Muscovy ducks, if only Dan would get round to making the pool. Mike had a farmer friend who had a collection of wild-fowl as well as the more exotic farmyard birds. There were two beautiful Chinese cocks and two hens, if Anna would like some fancy poultry. But Anna had decided it was time to call a stop. She already had her hands full.

Only three more days to Easter and Phil and Lisa would be home. They would love the pups, and soon after that there was a small show which would be fun to enter and would give them experience. Mike brought her the entry forms and she put the three in the puppy class for Alsatians. She was sure at least one of them would gain a place; probably Astro. He was growing fast. If only those ears would stay up. They gave him a lovely expression, but he needed erect ears. Otherwise she couldn't fault him, no matter how she tried.

'I never thought life could be so good again,' she said one morning at breakfast, looking out at the garden which was beginning to take shape. Dan had planted shrubs against the fence and softened the starkness, and the day before he had begun on the pool. Mike had promised to bring the ducks as soon as they were ready.

Dan crossed his fingers. He never trusted luck. Life had run too smoothly for too long. There must be a cloud on the horizon. It wasn't possible that they could go on without a hitch.

He went out to the puppies and then wondered if he had brought ill luck on them by his own gloomy thoughts, for Amba lay miserably in the corner of her kennel and barely lifted her head to greet him, and it was very plain indeed that all was far from well.

CHAPTER TEN

Scott was baffled. Amba's symptoms were very odd. The vomiting and enteritis were common to many illnesses, but there was more to this than just that. Yet he didn't know what. He asked Anna to keep an eye on the two dog puppies. It could perhaps be a virus, or maybe a chill from the pond, as all three had been half soaked when she put them in the kennels. She had dried them off as best she could, but maybe she hadn't done it properly. Amba did not want to eat. She lay under her bench instead of on top of it, and did not move her head or wag her tail when Anna spoke. Scott gave her an injection.

'I'll be back in the morning,' he promised. 'Meanwhile, keep her warm.'

Dan moved the big oil heater and lit it. It had warmed a large henhouse and would warm the kennel block. Luckily he had built the block with a wide passage and a central area where he could store food, and there was plenty of space. Anna made up glucose and water and Dan fed the bitch with it, using a cattle hypodermic as a feeder. Amba lay without caring. It was too much effort to move, and she felt so very ill.

'It would be now, with the children coming home,' Anna said. Things never went wrong when it was convenient. She had extra shopping to do, and the furniture for Lisetta's room had not arrived. Heaven knew why. The shop kept promising, but promises seemed to be all that were forthcoming and Lisetta couldn't sleep on them. Dan bought a small camp bed. Anna had so wanted the room to be ready and to be a surprise, and now it would take away half the fun.

Phil's room was ready. He had a bunk bed built into a cupboard and Dan had spent hours making the room as exciting as was possible for any boy. Phil would love it and Lisa would be aggrieved. Would be sure they hadn't tried, would accuse them angrily of not bothering. Anna knew her daughter only too well.

Len brought Susan to visit, but took her away again when he heard that Amba was ill.

'Would you like me to come and look after the pups?' he asked.

Dan was about to say there was no need, but Anna, once more, noticed the wistfulness in the old man's voice and flashed a look at her husband. Men could be so very obtuse. And what was more she could do with help. She would soon be cooking nonstop. Phil had an appetite like a starving wolf. Though maybe Phil would help. Lisa wouldn't. She would be out with the horses, or having a bath, or washing her hair, or lost in a book. Goodness knows what she found to do but she was always busy with, apparently, nothing to show for it.

By morning Amba was eating again, but without much interest, and Argon was ill. Scott came back and gave both pups injections. He spent some time with the little bitch, frowning and intent. Anna felt her hopes go tumbling. She had wanted so much to start breeding and an illness now might affect all the future.

These pups were good pups. Mike Redwood had brought two friends of his to see them, and one of the men had offered her one hundred and fifty pounds for Astro. It was very tempting, but she wanted him for herself. She never told Dan. Money was becoming a problem. The horse field had been inadequately fenced and the cost of new fencing had been prohibitive. They rented it from the farmer but he refused to fence. The horses were not his. They were Dan's responsibility. She still shivered when she thought of the cost of the fence. And they had had to buy in extra hay as the first lot had been such poor quality that Dan refused to feed it to the horses. He spent a week touring farms before he found any that was good enough. Trust a farmer to know good hay, Len had said when he saw the new stack, and had nodded approvingly.

Len was coming every day, spending all day with the pups, giving glucose and water every hour. Amba was listless and had no desire to run or play, and Argon was very ill indeed. So ill that when Scott came he said that Anna would have to spend the night with the pup, to keep him warm and to give him glucose. By the time that Phil and Lisa were due she was feeling sick with worry, and Astro too was refusing to eat. She wished that her son and daughter were not coming, and then felt guilty so that she snapped at Dan, who was anxious himself and shouted at her.

'Hey, hey,' Len said, coming in to the kitchen for more glucose. 'I reckon those pups got chilled. They'll be all right. Pups are hardy little things.'

'We should have left them in the whelping kennel where it was warm,' Anna said irritably. 'The big block's too cold for them. They were all right until we moved them.'

'They've been there nearly four weeks,' Dan said. 'They'd have shown signs before if it was chilling from the kennels. And it's much warmer now than it has been.'

Anna had no answer. She hated any animal being ill, hated the forlorn look in the little beasts' eyes. They didn't know what had hit them. These pups had never known a day's illness before, and neither inoculations nor worming had upset them.

Phil and Lisa arrived but were not allowed near the kennel block. They both hated Setter's Dene and agonised Anna by telling her about the new motorway and how Compton Hall had been knocked down in three days, and there was nothing left. Only the wide road stretching across the silent fields. Lisa hated her room; and was as furious as Anna had expected.

'You do everything for him and nothing for me. I don't matter, I'm just a girl. You would have to get his room ready first, wouldn't you?'

Anna gave up. It was no use arguing and Len had just come in to ask her to ring Scott and then come and look at Astro, who was behaving very oddly indeed. His eyes were twitching. Scott promised to come at once and Anna went in to the kennels. Argon had begun to pick up after his injection, but Astro lay quiet and was very hot. Len had covered the pup with a blanket and was sitting on the bench, watching him. All the pups had crawled to the floor and crept under their benches into the dark.

'I'll stay here all night,' Len said. 'I can sleep in the daytime and no one will worry me. Maybe those kids of yours could go and see young Susan. She'll be missing me.'

Much to Anna's relief, Lisetta immediately took charge of Susie, bringing her home to play with the cats and to talk to the horses, more gentle than either Dan or his wife would have believed possible. Phil took the little girl for a walk in the woods, promising to see that she did not trip up or bump into anything. Susan's mother was anxious at first, but after several expeditions she relaxed, and Susie, sitting at tea with Lisa and Phil, chattered more than Anna had ever heard her, and told them a long story about a witch and black cat and put all of Anna's animals into it.

'When I learn Braille properly, I'm going to be a writer,' Susie said. She was sitting on the settee, Zelie close against her and Soot on her lap. She had no fear of any of the animals now, and loved Zelie, who treated the little blind girl as if she were one of her own pups, in need of a mother's care. Several times Anna had wondered if the bitch realised the child was blind, as now, if Susan took hold of Zelie's collar, the Alsatian would lead her outside as safely as if she had been taught, and Susie was delighted and, provided Dan or Len or Anna was near, would follow the bitch into the garden and walk about in the sunshine.

The game so interested Phil and Lisa that they made a special harness of two leads and encouraged Zelie to lead Susan all over the house and garden. Anna watched. Her interest was roused, but her mind was on the pups. They were all three better, but none of them was well. They acted oddly and were listless, and all of them began to whine and whimper constantly for no reason at all.

Anna was very glad when it was time for the children to return to school. She needed to get the puppies fit again. And she knew that Scott was disturbed. He called in daily, not officially, but begging for coffee, as he was passing, and always went out to the kennel block to have a look at the three.

'They aren't right, are they?' Anna asked.

'I can't think what's wrong,' Scott said. 'I've been asking all my friends, and none of them knows of a virus with symptoms like this. I thought it might be distemper, but it's not that. And it's not from chilling. That might have started off the attack, but it's not the cause of the trouble now. They aren't exactly ill,' he added hastily, seeing Anna's face.

'And they're not well,' Anna said.

Not even Amba greeted her with fervour now. The little bitch had lost all her merriness and when Anna took her out, she plodded meekly along, without any savour or sparkle. The dogs were as bad.

And then, quite suddenly, after Phil and Lisa had returned to school, they began to pick up, to eat their food with interest, to run and play again. Anna let them into the garden and watched them chase one another, and roll and snarl in mock fights. Amba ran to her and leaped up, leaving muddy paw marks all over her clothes, and Argon leaned against her. His head was broadening and he was growing, although his illness had checked him. Astro was undoubtedly making a very handsome pup, if only his ears would stay up. They seemed to have a life of their own, and though he could perk them up and one or the other would go erect, he usually sat in an amiable puppy sprawl with both ears down and an endearing expression on his face. He was chattier than ever, and all of them seemed to squeal much more than they had before they were ill. But perhaps that was only because they were growing up, and pups were excitable.

By the time May was well advanced, Mike was visiting regularly, talking about their first Show, and there was a tacit agreement that he should handle them. Anna and Len and Mike walked one puppy each and often ended in the local inn, a delightful friendly little place called the Heart of Oak, where Jenny and Ron Martin both had dogs of their own and welcomed dog owners. Scott often joined them, and Dan came too when he had time, but he was now finishing off the pool and installing a pen for the ducks, so that the dogs could not get at them, and he begrudged every minute.

Anna loved the Heart of Oak. The long room with its padded benches was comfortable and homely, warmed by an immense log fire at one end. There were horse brasses on the walls, and a large bowl of water for visiting dogs on the floor, and a fire-screen with a mirror edge in which Amba saw four puppies watching her and sat, astounded at such a sight, especially as the puppies kept moving but had no smell.

Here all of them went, with the dogs, on Anna's birthday at the end of May. The pups seemed quite recovered, except for the frequent whining, and Mike had entry forms for a small local Show which would give them experience. Scott treated everyone to baked bean toasties and pints of bitter, while Anna chose lager and lime, and watched the sun gild the empty fireplace, and watched the pups' alert ears as people came and went about them, often stopping to speak to them and stroke them and admire them. She wondered how she had ever imagined this was an unfriendly place.

'Drinks all round,' a newcomer said excitedly as he erupted into the room, the door swinging behind him.

'How'd it go, Joe?' asked someone in the corner.

Joe was a sombrely dressed man, his body too fat, his legs thick and solid in tight trousers. His red face was beaming as he surveyed the onlookers.

'I got thirty thousand pounds for it,' he said. 'Thirty thousand; they must be mad.'

'Joe's moving in with his son, down South. He bought his cottage for six thousand pounds ten years ago and they auctioned it this morning,' Len said. 'Ee, they'll be selling that shed down Sally Street for ten thousand next. Thirty thousand!'

Knowing what he had paid for his two cottages, Dan wasn't surprised. Prices were going haywire. And he'd been told, only today, that horse feed and dog feed would be going up in price. Life became a desperate race to keep up with yourself all the time. He'd have to start kennelling boarders and he'd have to charge a pound a day at least to make a profit. And if he didn't make a profit they couldn't keep on. And if they didn't keep on life wouldn't be worth living, so what did a man do?

He lifted his glass.

'Happy birthday,' he said, to change the drift of his thoughts, and Anna smiled at him. She turned to look at the pups. Nothing wrong with them now. They looked supremely fit. Mike caught her glance.

'I'll bet you a tenner to a glass of ale that Astro's the best of that bunch,' he said.

Anna shook her head.

'Argon's my pup,' she said with conviction. 'Look at him.'

'Head's too narrow,' said Mike. 'Look at Astro. You can't fault him.'

'His ears won't stay up,' Anna said.

'They will. When he's ready. They often don't come up till six months. He's splendidly made. A beautiful pup.'

"So is Amba,' Len said. The little bitch was always his favourite. She heard her name and wagged her tail and stood up and licked him. He laughed and pushed her down again.

'It's like a madhouse in here,' Ron said, as he collected the glasses and patted the dogs. 'It's time, I'm afraid.'

Time had gone speeding fast. Outside, in the car park, in the sunshine, Mike walked each pup in turn, and then Anna took them, admiring their action, the way each moved, the fine way each pup stood.

'They'll win every time you put them in,' Mike said.

'Both dogs can't win,' Anna answered, and walked off up the hill, excitement building in her again. It was impossible not to dream, not to build castles in the air, not to bank on putting red rosettes for the dogs beside the rosettes on the dresser; to start winning again at the Shows, even if it wasn't with cattle.

She went indoors, leaving the pups in their kennels, and made coffee for the men. Scott had a surgery to take and left them, flashing past in his sports car, but Len and Dan and Mike had time to spare, and Susie's mother had made Anna a birthday cake. Later on, Len was going back to fetch the child for a birthday tea. Anna had not felt so happy since she had left Compton Hall. She poured coffee and cut the cake.

Zelie was lying in the sunshine with Soot beside her. The old man's two cats, Black and Tan, were curled on the window-sill. Smoke was lying under one of the lavender bushes that Dan had planted beside the path. There were horses in the field, grazing. Suntan and Razzle had now been accepted and joined them. It was easier with four. They seemed to pair off, and there were two heads at one end of the field and two at the other. The goats were tethered on the grass. Yodel had been sold.

Sunshine spilled across the beds of annuals that Dan had put in for her. There were pansies alongside the house, yellow and purple with black centres, and little bachelor's buttons, and a bed of vivid wallflowers, now almost over. Len had been helping with the garden too. Their coming had been a godsend for the old man.

Zelie lifted her head. The cats sat up and stared, and the two goats tugged at the tethers. The eeriest noise was coming from the kennel block.

Everyone ran.

Little Astro was squealing. He raced round and round his kennel, pushing his head under the bench, trying to hide in the dark corners, totally berserk. Mike pushed open the door and went inside, and the pup rushed at him, mouth wide and snarling. Mike leaped out and slammed the door shut. The pup hit the door and dropped to the ground, exhausted.

Dan pushed the door open and went inside to pick the little animal up and put him on his sleeping bench, out of the draught.

'What the hell did that?' Mike said.

Dan was standing facing them; Astro in his arms. He looked at Anna, stricken.

'Your pup's dead,' he said.

Dead? Anna could not believe him, but it was quite true. There would never by any prizes for Astro.

She went outside, unable to speak to any of them. Unbelievably, the sun was still shining.

CHAPTER ELEVEN

It was a disastrous birthday tea. Susan was inconsolable. Astro had been 'her' pup. He had been her favourite, and she had adored him. Anna drank three cups of tea without even tasting them. Dan telephoned Scott and came back, saying nothing. Mike stayed on, not knowing what to say either. There was nothing he could say.

Anna's thoughts raced round and round. Supposing it was a relapse from the illness they had all had? Were the other pups going to drop dead too? Would she have to start again, right from the very beginning, looking for pups that would have the qualities she wanted? Zelie's had been so perfect in every way. She could buy in two older Alsatians but she didn't want to. She wanted to rear her own litter. She liked having pups about the place, and also she liked to know what had happened to them before she began to breed. A bad past could affect the whole future. And there were not many animals like Zelie.

An ill-treated bitch might never settle to maternity; might attack her puppies; might attack her owner if she guarded them too fiercely and she hadn't been handled properly right from the start. It was so easy to ruin a good-tempered dog by stupid treatment; to let it play rough and boss the family and take over from them. Scott was always complaining about the number of dogs that came to him for treatment with owners that were obviously slightly scared of their pets and expected to be bitten, and were. No one had ever shown the dog just who was boss. And the dog was boss. It was as simple as that, and Anna wasn't having any boss dogs in her household.

Scott came and examined Astro and took his body away for a post mortem. It was important to find out just how he had died. If it was from a bug, Zelie and Zinta and the other two pups were at risk. He was still mystified. The symptoms were so extraordinary and he had never seen anything like them. He went away with worrying thoughts of a new epidemic, previously unknown in this country. People smuggled in dogs; perhaps it had been brought that way. The quarantine laws were only too necessary.

The week dragged past. Anna was reluctant to open the kennels in the morning lest Amba and Argon were also dead. But both regained their spirits and greeted her with wild joy, racing at the wire door, standing on hind legs, desperate to greet her with wildly licking tongues and madly wagging tails.

Amba, taken out of her kennel, behaved like a seal and swam around the grass, delirious with excitement at being free. It was always some minutes before she recovered and stood up and was a dog again. It never failed to make Anna laugh, but fear lay behind the laughter and she found herself looking for symptoms; listening for a high-pitched hysterical note in their squeals of welcome, running to the kennels at the least unusual sound, watching out for enteritis and vomiting.

Meanwhile, Scott called and looked at the pups, and rang the Ministry laboratory daily to see if the tests had been completed.

Nothing.

No sign of disease.

No sign of infection.

Not one single suggestive clue as to why Astro had died. Anna felt desperate. He couldn't have died of nothing. His heart was sound and there was no sign of brain damage.

'I've got an idea,' Scott said on the sixth afternoon, while drinking coffee in Anna's big living-room, with Black sprawled across his lap and Tan sitting close against him. Both cats adored him, and Smoke became jealous and took herself off to the windowsill and sat there, eyeing them inimically.

But he refused to tell her his idea, and she waited miserably.

'If only we knew,' she said for the hundredth time to Dan.

'You've been a farmer's wife for long enough to know there are always mysteries,' Dan said on the seventh afternoon after Astro's death. Scott had telephoned to say he was coming to see them after surgery, and Anna put the coffee on to percolate, knowing the vet liked his black and strong and in the biggest available cup.

'I never get used to it,' Anna said.

'There was Gillie . . . do you remember? She died in the night during the foot-and-mouth epidemic, and we had a panic. Jack never did find out what was wrong. And the calves that died overnight, inexplicably. Fine in the evening and dead by morning. And the pigs and chicks we lost. There's always danger with young stock. You'll have to get used to it. You can't expect to rear every pup.'

'I don't,' Anna said. 'But I don't expect to lose them without a reason when they're more than four months old. They usually die in the first few days. And these were such sturdy pups. They've never had a thing wrong with them till now, and I'm sure it's all connected.'

And I'm not sure the other two will survive, she thought miserably. But she did not say it aloud. Never count your apples. She had. It didn't do. She would soon be as superstitious as Dan and his father, and she had always laughed at them. She would never make plans again. Never live beyond the immediate day. Never count on tomorrow. It didn't always come. No tomorrow for Astro.

She was getting morbid. She went outside and milked the goats. It was relaxing and soothing and took her mind off the pups. She had just finished and brought the pail inside and was making up Zinta's feed when Scott arrived.

He came into the kitchen, stooping to avoid the low beam that was just inside the door. The cottages were Victorian and not so very old, but somebody had strengthened the kitchen ceiling so that the bath could stand safely overhead. There had been a vast old iron bath when they first saw the place, but they had replaced it with more modern bathroom furniture.

'I've got your answer,' Scott said as he took the mug of coffee. 'And it's going to leave us with a puzzle. Astro died of lead poisoning.'

'Lead poisoning?' Dan said. 'How in God's name did he get that? And what about the other two?'

'They've got it too, but obviously not so badly,' Scott said. 'The pup had twenty parts per million in his liver and fifteen parts in his kidneys, and about five parts is a lethal dose. No wonder he died. The question is, where has it come from?'

'And what about Argon and Amba?' Anna said, the most important part of the problem foremost in her mind.

'There's an antidote,' Scott answered. 'They seem all right, so I'll drive over and get it tonight to save waiting for the postal delivery which might take any time. And inject it tomorrow. They seem fine and the symptoms aren't too prominent so we'll just have to hope. But I can't promise anything.'

'What are the symptoms?' Anna asked.

'Extreme thirst. The original diarrhoea and vomiting that they had. That hysterical squealing. And the pups try to get their heads in the dark. I don't know if they become light sensitive. That's what Astro was trying to do when he was racing around. To get out of the light. That's why they crawl under their benches instead of lying on top of them like any

104

normal pup. But at least we know. The next thing we must do is find out how they got it.'

'It could be water,' Dan said. 'I haven't examined the pipes here. It never occurred to me. The cottages are old enough to still have lead piping.'

'I'd get the Water Board to check,' Scott said. 'I'll ring them for you. For one thing, you're at risk too if it's the water pipes. Lead's a slow poison. It accumulates over a period, and only builds up gradually to a lethal dose. It could come from paint. Children die from sucking painted toys from abroad. The lead compound that's used in paint is sweet and they get a craving for it and become addicted. There were ten calves that died from licking tins of paint abandoned on a waste tip near a farm I visit, only last year. Old paint, banned nowadays, thrown out by the painter, but when it was dumped the lids came off and the cattle went crazy for it. It was several days before we found out why they died, and we didn't see any symptoms as that was a massive dosage and they died in the night.'

'There could have been lead paint on the shippons at home,' Anna said. 'We lost calves for no explicable reason and it costs too much to have post mortems on all of them. Maybe lead accounts for a lot of cases of calf scour.'

'There's no old paint here, though, is there?' Scott asked. 'Your kennels are brand-new, aren't they?'

'They're made of second-hand wood,' Dan said. 'The paint was so good that I only cleaned it up. I didn't repaint. I was going to do that later. There's so much to be done. I never even thought of lead paint. Not nowadays. But the wood came from a demolished building.'

'I've a friend who can analyse that paint for you,' Len said. He had come in while they were talking, having free access to the house. Anna didn't know how she had ever done without him. He poured himself a cup of coffee and sat quietly listening to the conversation and she had not noticed he was there. Her attention had been on Scott.

Trust Len to know someone. He seemed to have all kinds of contacts, having lived his whole life in the village. There still was a village, she had discovered, in spite of the new estates, keeping itself to itself and living an oddly vigorous country life in the middle of suburbia. It was impossible now to remember the first lonely days at Setter's Dene. She seemed to have acquired a totally new household and to have as many visitors as she had had at Compton Hall. There would be more when the children came home for good. Susan came daily, as she was promised one of Zinta's pups for her own to make up for losing Astro, and she was waiting anxiously.

Scott rang the Water Board from Setter's Dene. They promised to come at once and check all the pipes. It was a dangerous situation, and both Anna and Dan felt nervous, wondering if they too were suffering from lead poisoning. It caused unpredictable irritability and Anna certainly felt edgier than usual. But she had enough cause, she thought, as she fed Zinta and took Zelie out for exercise, and left Len to let the pups out into the garden and romp together. Dan had gone back to planting round the pool. He had dredged out the mud and the water lay cool and clear and attractive beyond the kennel block.

The little corner was sheltered from the wind. Len had promised to plant a hedge to hide the kennels and make her a little garden where she could sit in the summer. If she ever had time. She was already busier than she had expected and, oddly, a small house was much harder to keep clean than a large one. The dirt brought in from outside all seemed to be concentrated in the kitchen. She had to scrub the floor twice a day or mud was trampled in on the carpets.

Soot added to her problems by becoming a champion bird catcher. Anna was forever rescuing his prey from him and giving it to Len to nurse back to health. Soot had grown into a very handsome little cat, and Scott had neutered him and spayed Smoke. Anna couldn't face any more kittens. She had more than enough to do and at times wondered how on earth she had coped at Compton Hall with farm life, and pigs and chickens to tend. Len kept chickens and brought her eggs every week, and she supplied him with goat's milk. He refused all payment for looking after the dogs, explaining that he did it for his own pleasure, and it did him good.

It did, too, Anna thought, watching the old man as he played ball with the pups. They had a big football which they adored, batting it to and fro between themselves, sending it now and again to Len who kicked it for them to chase. He had a broad grin on his face as he watched them, and nowadays often whistled to himself, more than delighted to be doing something useful again.

He walked towards Anna as she came in through the gate with Zelie.

'We should get the result on that paint tonight,' he said. 'Tom says he'll meet me in the Heart at opening time. If it's the paint we'd better get the stuff off the kennels quick and put the pups somewhere else. It's a funny old do, right enough.'

Funny was the understatement of the year, Anna thought, and watched Zelie greet the pups enthusiastically. Amba adored her mother and rushed up to her and licked her face, and Zelie bent her head to lick her daughter. Anna watched them, feeling happier than she had done since Astro died. The pups were both looking fine.

Len whistled to them. Both came when he called. He spent a lot of time with them. His old Lass was getting too old to walk far now and spent much of her time lying outside his cottage on the porch. He went home at frequent intervals to exercise and feed her, as he gave her several small meals every day. Her digestion was faulty too.

'I'll have to take her to the vet,' he had said mournfully to Anna only a few days before, and Anna mentally reserved one of Zinta's pups for the old man. More profit gone, but he'd done so much for her that she couldn't grudge it him. He was worth several pounds a week in wages and he would never take a penny.

She watched him walk towards the kennel block. The two pups were following, knowing that they would be fed. He might be old, but he was a very hale man and would easily live to a hundred, Anna thought. He was one of those wiry little men who seemed able to go on for ever.

Len and the pups vanished. Anna whistled Zelie and turned to go indoors. She was just entering the kitchen door when the squealing began. She turned and raced towards the kennels just as Len came out, his face sombre.

'It's Argon. Just like Astro,' he said.

'Let's leave him and ring Scott. If only he isn't halfway to wherever he has to go to get the antidote.' She ran indoors, and Len shut the kennel block up. There was nothing he could do and maybe the pup was better left on his own. If only Scott was in.

Scott was not in. His wife didn't know when he'd be back but suggested that Anna rang another vet who sometimes acted as stand-in and tell him just what was wrong. Scott had driven off to get the antidote from a laboratory fifteen miles away. She'd tell him at once, as soon as he got back.

Anna thanked her, rang off, and dialled again. The bell seemed to go on ringing endlessly, but at last there was an answer. Anna gave her name.

'You own the pups that have lead poisoning,' the man at the other end of the line said, and she breathed a deep sigh of relief. At least she didn't have to explain.

'The other dog puppy has just started squealing hysterically, exactly like his brother,' she said.

'Shut him in the dark,' the voice ordered. 'Don't go near him. Or near any other dog in the kennels. Death can be triggered by excitement and if you leave him entirely alone he may quieten down. It's his only chance. There's nothing else you can do until you get the antidote.'

Anna rang off and told Len what they had to do. They sat helplessly looking at one another. The squealing continued on a high-pitched frantic note, and Amba joined in. Anna listened, but Amba was barking, not squealing. They ought to move her, but Argon needed to be left alone. She would have to take her chance. Zelie was uneasy, walking to the window, pawing at Anna, bothered by the noise, and outside in the whelping kennel Zinta began to howl, a high-pitched horrible eerie noise that went on and on in tune with Argon's screaming. If only he wasn't racing round the kennel. Suppose he injured himself.

Suppose he dropped dead. Astro had squealed for ten minutes. Anna looked at the clock, which appeared to have stopped. Argon had already been squealing for more than twenty minutes. There was a pause in the noise. A moment's pause. Time for her heart to stop racing and then to start pounding again. Supposing he was dead? If only he'd start again. She would welcome the noise. At least it would show that he was alive.

She'd been very fond of Astro and very sad when he died, but she'd set her heart on Argon. He was a lovely dog, with a wonderful nature, gentle and biddable, easy to teach, walking at heel, understanding the commands that were given him. Amba was sweet, but it was Dan who counted in the little bitch's life. She adored him. If only Argon would howl again.

Dan came in and looked at them.

'You look like a wake,' he said.

109

'I feel like a wake,' Anna said. 'Didn't you hear Argon just now?'

'I heard all the dogs,' Dan said. 'And thought it was a very good job we haven't any near neighbours.'

'He was squealing just like Astro,' Len said.

'He's dead,' Anna said, and then sighed deeply as the squealing began again. He wasn't dead. He was still making a horrible noise, and he would soon be exhausted. And then what? Amba began to bark in unison, and Zinta started to howl again. Len made tea, but nobody drank it. The cups went cold as they sat and listened.

'If only Scott would come,' Anna said. 'He doesn't know there's any hurry. And we can't get in touch with him, I don't know where he's gone.'

The shrilling phone bell startled all of them. Anna went to answer it, barely able to hear for the noise the dogs were making.

'Anna? It's Scott here. I'm at the laboratory. My wife left a message. Is Argon still squealing?'

'Yes,' Anna said. If only he wouldn't stop. She'd never dare go and see what had happened. She couldn't bear the thought of losing him as well as Astro. Not so soon. Not when life was beginning to have some point again. Not when she was forgetting about Compton Hall and recovering from her misery. She couldn't lose Argon too.

'I'm on my way,' Scott said.

'Be careful.' Anna couldn't bear the thought of anything happening to delay him.

Len had made a second pot of tea.

'Come on, Missus. It'll do you good. We can't change what's going to happen, not now. Maybe the pup will get over it. He's been in fine shape, anyone could see that, and Astro was very much worse than either of them two when he was ill.'

Anna drank her tea without tasting it. She couldn't stop looking at the clock. How long did it take to drive fifteen miles?

'It's rush hour,' Len said, seeing her glance.

'They've stopped,' Dan said.

It was more than she could bear. Suppose she went to look? To see if the pup was still alive; to make sure that Amba was barking and not squealing too. Suppose both of them died just before Scott brought the anitdote? She began to feel sick and could not listen to either Dan or Len who had begun a long and involved argument about the best way to get the paint off the kennels if that was the cause of the trouble. Luckily they hadn't used the same wood for the whelping kennel. That was unpainted, and so Zelie and Zinta were safe. Unless it was the water.

'Here we go round the mulberry bush,' Anna said drearily. She lifted her head at the sound of an engine, but it was the first car of the evening rush hour passing their gate.

The squealing began again.

He was still alive. But how long could he last? And what use would the antidote be now? Did it act as quickly as that? If only Scott would come.

'I reckon if vet don't come, it'll be too late,' Len said, and stood up to go home. 'Got to face facts, Missus. That pup won't have any strength left.'

The squealing was fainter now, was a thin echo of sound, fading and rising and tailing off again, with long silences between. Each time he started, the other dogs followed. It was bad for Zinta. Anna did not know what to do with her. Zelie would never allow her indoors and Zelie herself was upset and couldn't be left by herself. Even the cats were distraught and had curled together in a huddle, gazing with worried eyes out of the window, as if trying to find out what was making the noise.

There was a thump on the back door, and as it opened a voice called out.

'Only me. Any coffee?'

It was Mike Redwood. He came through into the living-room, his face concerned.

'That's a bloody funny noise. Sounds like a wolf dying. Who's making it?'

'Argon. Astro died of lead poisoning. The other two have it as well, and Scott's gone for the antidote. He's not going to be in time,' Anna said.

Mike poured himself a cup of coffee.

'Join the wake.' Dan had walked to the window and was looking out, chinking the coins in his pocket. Anna suddenly thought that if one more person came and asked her what was wrong, she would scream. It was a good job Susan had a bad cold and wouldn't be visiting for several days. It was a good job Zinta hadn't had her pups yet, thought by the way she was barking they would be brought on early.

Over two hours since Argon had started squealing.

She sat down again, helplessly, and picked up a book, but the words made no sense.

Outside, in the kennels, the barking and squealing went on. And on. And on.

There was no conceivable hope left.

Scott was going to be too late.

CHAPTER TWELVE

There had been no sounds for fifteen minutes before Scott arrived. Anna heard his tyres screech as he braked. He came swiftly up the drive.

'He's dead,' she said drearily.

'Have you been to see?' Scott asked.

Anna shook her head, and at the same moment the squealing began again. She looked shakily at the vet.

'Do you think the antidote will do any good?' she asked.

'It's impossible to say.' Scott was already walking down the path to the kennels, with Dan and Mike beside him. Anna went indoors and cleared up the cups and washed them up, and took Zinta her food, and fed the cats, and Zelie. There was food ready for both the pups, but she didn't feel they should have it now.

There was a sudden savage barking from the kennels and then complete silence. Anna wanted to go and look, and yet she did not dare. She began to clean the kitchen windows, which were already sparkling. She had to do something, anything, to distract herself. All that work and money wasted, never mind anything else. Dan had said the antidote, which was a mixture of some calcium salt and saline, was as much of a shock to the pups' system as the original poisoning. They might not survive the night, even if they were alive now.

There were footsteps on the path.

Anna looked out of the window and knew that everything was just as bad as she had feared. Dan was carrying Argon's body. The pup was dead. She only had Amba left. She turned away from the window, a lump thickening her throat and tears scalding her eyes.

'We had to give him an anaesthetic,' Scott's voice said just behind her. 'It's a difficult injection, and I've put him right out. I want him kept warm, so he'd better come into the house for the night. He's pretty exhausted, so he'll need careful nursing.'

'He isn't dead?' Anna couldn't believe it. She had made up her mind to believe the worst. She saw the pup's chest move as he breathed, and practicality reasserted itself. She put blankets down against the radiator and Dan covered the pup.

'We'll put him in Lisa's room for the night,' he said. The furniture still hadn't arrived. Dan had phoned several times and been into the shop twice, but no one could hurry the manufacturers. Anna wondered if the room would be ready when Lisa came home for good.

It was difficult to concentrate on anything. Her mind was on the dogs. There was no sign of movement from Argon, but Amba, who had had less anaesthetic and had not spent the day squealing hysterically, was on her feet by eight o'clock, demanding the food that she had missed. Anna watched the pup eat. She seemed no worse for the injection, or the anaesthetic. She stood on her hind legs, both paws against Anna's shoulders, and then sealed across the floor, playing the fool. Anna knelt to stroke the little bitch. If only they survived. She seemed all right, but so had Astro, and Argon had been as fit as any dog could be up to that morning.

Len came by on his way home to supper.

'It's the paint all right,' he said. 'Eighty per cent lead. No wonder they took sick. It's a miracle they're still alive.'

'Then for heaven's sake get Amba out of her kennel,' Anna said. 'She can't stay there. She's reinfecting herself. They must be licking it.'

'They'll be standing up and scratching it with their paws, and the flakes'll fall on the floor,' Len said. 'Then they eat it when they eat their paunch. Drag that stuff all over the place, they do.' All Anna's dogs adored raw paunch and were given large pieces to tear and worry at. Argon alway took his on to his bench, but Amba chased hers round the floor, revelling in every delectable mouthful.

Dan moved Amba into a stall in the goat shed. Tomorrow he would strip off all the paint, all over the kennels, burning down to the wood, scraping, and repainting. And he'd make quite sure the new paint had no lead in it. Old sins cast long shadows. He patted the little bitch as she settled in for the night.

'She seems fine,' he commented. He had not told Anna that Argon had gone berserk when they opened his kennel and they had had to give him an enormous amount of anaesthetic as a result. There was no need to worry her about that. But Dan kept checking, all the same, bending over the dog to make sure he was still breathing.

It was almost bedtime before Argon showed signs of life. He opened his eyes and looked about him. He was in a strange place and felt extremely odd, but Dan and Anna were there, and Zelie was lying beside him. He wagged his tail and the thump against the wood brought Anna over to look at him. He licked her hand, and she went down on her knees beside him. He seemed none the worse for his experiences.

'If only he survives the night . . .' Anna said.

'I don't think I'll move him after all,' Dan said. 'You go to bed and I'll sit up until three. Then you can take over and sleep on in the morning.'

'I'll never sleep.'

Anna was convinced, but for all that the day had exhausted her and she slept at once, waking wearily, struggling into jeans and jersey when the alarm-clock went.

Argon wagged his tail as she walked into the room.

Dan lifted both hands, his fingers crossed.

'Never count apples,' he said, 'but . . .'

It was difficult not to hope. By morning no one would have guessed that anything had ever been wrong with either pup. They were ravenous, and Anna fed them and put them together in the goat shed, while Dan started on the kennels.

Five minutes later she hurtled outside at the sound of vicious fighting. She opened the shed door. The two pups were at one another's throats. Dan raced down the path and rushed into the kennel, needing all his strength to separate them. He slammed the door shut, leaving Argon inside and

Amba outside. She wagged her tail, sealed down the path and went to greet Zelie.

'They can't be put together any more,' Dan said. 'They meant that. I wonder if the poisoning has affected their personal smells? I don't see why they should fight.'

'Litter domination,' Len said. He had come up the path as Dan slammed the door shut. 'You'll find the bitch wants to be boss and maybe you've got a bold dog there who won't let her. So they'll fight it out to see who's going to win.'

'That means they can't be kennelled together or exercised together,' Anna said. And that would be a nuisance as it would mean double exercise for her.

'They'll be OK outside,' Len said positively. 'It's only on home ground that they'll fight. You'll still be able to walk them together. Looks like they've taken the antidote well.'

Anna had given up planning. One day at a time was all she asked. One day nearer to safety. One more day and the poison must surely be worked out of their systems. And Amba had not shown any signs of hysteria. So Amba at least was safe. Every time Argon barked she listened to the sound he made. There was never any mistaking that awful squeal. And it came again, but only briefly.

The days passed slowly. The pups had to be kept quiet. Scott gave both another dose of the antidote; the Water Board discovered that the pipes were lead; men came to lay new ones of copper. Dan stripped the kennels and painted them again, and the pups went back inside, this time well separated. Two dogs came to board.

Summer was coming and soon the pups could be shown. If only she dared hope, but Scott still refused to give her certainty. No one knew anything about after symptoms and so few animals survived and he could find nothing helpful in the literature he had searched through. He had questioned all his friends,

116

had written to his old university, but no one had any experience of animals that had recovered from such a disaster. It seemed the pups were unique.

Summer came and the gardens at the end of the lane were brilliant with flowers. Trees massed with blossom lined the streets beyond, and yellow laburnum pendants hung in almost every drive. Cheshire was a county of gardeners.

There were Muscovy ducks on the pool. A moorhen had hatched out a brood in the rushes that had grown thickly when Dan had finished clearing the ground. The chicks were hand tame. Anna spent some of her time kneeling by the pool with Susan beside her, coaxing them to come for crumbs. Soon they allowed the blind child to approach them. Anna never ceased to marvel at the gentle sensitive fingers, which had a life of their own, not needing eyes to show Susan how to touch without rousing fear. Both Argon and Amba stood quiet to let her fondle them, and Zelie and Zinta knew that they must not jump or move roughly when she was near.

Zinta had six pups, four of them longhairs, which Anna could not sell for as much as she had hoped. She was already out of pocket on that particular boarder. As soon as all the pups were weaned the Alsatian could return home.

One bright morning in May, Scott called for coffee. It was Susan's eleventh birthday next week and Anna was giving a party, inviting the child's mother, and Len, and Mike Redwood, and Scott had promised to drop in for a few minutes if he were free.

'Mike's a good bloke,' Scott said. 'Why don't you put the pups in for the local Show and let him handle them? He'll do it for free, this time, as they haven't been ring trained. I was talking to him yesterday. He's sure those pups have a future, and you with them. You can trust him completely, he never did an underhand thing in his life. And he does know dogs. He's worked with them ever since he

117

grew up, and that was nearly forty years ago. He's trained them, and he used to run a beagle pack. He's done all kinds of things in his time.'

'Do you think the pups will be all right now?' Anna asked. So many people were anxious to tell her of the possible dire consequences of the poisoning; of bone damage, or damage that would prevent them breeding, or worse, of brain damage.

'They're all right,' Scott said. 'They've had enough antidote to remove a ton of lead. And the stuff's excreted. It must all be out of their system by now. If it wasn't, they'd still be whining and crying and trying to get out of the light and into the dark, and there's been no sign of that for some weeks now.'

It was more hopeful than she had expected. Scott had previously refused to commit himself at all. The pups had had blood tests to find out the lead levels in their blood, but they had been inconclusive, and no one knew if the poison could stay in their organs and not show up in the tests.

'They'll be all right now,' Scott said as he drove off. Anna watched him go. It was easy enough to say and they weren't his pups. She went over to look at them and was greeted vociferously by both. Zelie, jealous, came to look for her mistress and nosed her leg. She hated being left out, she had settled completely with no sign of regretting her old home, though she had pulled towards the gate when she had passed it a few days before. The cottage had been sold for a fortune. More than thirty thousand pounds. It was frightening to think of such an amount paid for a place that had been rented for only a few shillings and that needed work done on it. The builders had moved in and gutted the interior completely. All the woodwork lay in a rubbled pile in the orchard that was now bright with blossom. Anna sighed as she thought of the old man. She wished he had seen Zelie's pups and could know his beasts were well.

'This place must be worth a mint of money,' she said to Dan that night, and he nodded. 'It's not like Compton Hall, but it has its points.' They were standing outside in the little water garden where the ducks squabbled and waddled and dived for food. Mike Redwood had offered them a pair of Canada geese and was bringing them later that morning. For the first time, Anna felt a sudden surge of affection for her new home.

She remembered it on the morning of Susan's birthday, which kept up the fair weather promised by the barometer and the weather bureau. There was a new routine these days. Anna fed the goats and milked them and fed the dogs and cleaned the kennels and petted the boarders; at present she had a little Jack Russell terrier, who had brought his owner's glove with him and guarded it diligently; a slender whippet with abashed brown eyes and tucked-down tail and a nervous vibrant body that quivered whenever Anna spoke; and a young Dalmatian bitch that greeted everyone with all her body, wriggling from head to tail, her mouth agape.

There was endless interest in the visitors, though one of them, a Kerry Blue that had just gone home, had proved to have a most unpredictable temperament and only Dan had been able to handle him, except when Mike Redwood called. He could manage any dog. They all obeyed him, quelled at once by a look.

Len had the same quality but complained that it was deserting him.

'The shepherd's eye,' he said. 'You need it with dogs. Make up your mind to be boss. I miss old Lass,' he added. Lass had had to go a few weeks before. Life had become unendurable for her, as arthritis crippled her so badly she could barely move. He was taking one of Zinta's longhaired pups.

He came down on Susan's birthday to help Anna

with the dogs and to bring his own contribution to the day; a dozen fresh eggs.

'I still miss little Astro,' Anna said. 'It doesn't seem right even now to have two pups instead of three. I'm putting them in for the Show, Len.'

'Good,' Len said. 'Don't hope for too much, though. They won't do anything. Too green, but it's experience and will get them used to noise and people and to strange dogs and to judges and the ring. It's a lot for a pup to cope with, the first time. And these haven't really been places at all, as yet.'

There hadn't been time to take them about. Scott had only just decided that they could lead a normal life again. They had been kept quiet for so long. Anna watched them as they came headlong from the kennel and chased through the grass after Soot, who turned and slapped them both hard with his paw, one after the other, bringing them up standing. He often played with them and was quite unafraid, unlike Smoke who always fled. Black and Tan ignored them. Both cats were old and liked a sedentary existence, hunting out the sunniest patch in house or garden, and curling up to sleep.

'There's a car in the lane,' Anna said. An ancient Rolls pulled up outside. It was polished with so much vigour that the sun, reflecting from the paintwork, dazzled her. They rarely had strangers here. She went to the gate.

Inside were two men. The driver she recognised at once as the man who had been sweeping the drive at Sarvan Hall which she had visited with Tarquin, and then she recognised his passenger as the owner himself, muffled in scarves and a deerstalker hat, although the day was warm.

'I wanted to see what you had done with the cottages,' the old man said. 'Help me out, George.'

He moved slowly, and walked in through the open gateway. Len held both pups, having leashed them swiftly, recognising the visitor. He didn't want him

120

knocked over by boisterous dogs and this pair were lively and full of fun and lacked discipline as yet. Time to start teaching them again. He had had to stop while they were ill.

'They're nice pups,' the old man said. 'I heard about your bad luck. It seemed rather too much in such a short time.'

Anna led the way indoors.

'So you took my advice,' the old voice was soft, a dry whisper. 'You started again. And it's plain there's a good farmer running this place. It was totally derelict.'

'Started again?' Anna said, wondering what the old man had heard.

'Mike Redwood tells me you're going to breed Alsatians. Good ones. Doing it the right way, with the aim of improving the breed. He told me about your two pups and the lead poisoning. I've always had a passion for the breed, and I'd like to make a contribution myself. Too old now. But I could give you a stake.'

Anna looked at him, baffled. Was he offering to buy a partnership, or to give her some money, or what?

Mike Redwood came in at the door.

'So you beat me to it, Sir Joshua,' he said. 'I was afraid I'd get here first and steal your thunder.' He grinned at Anna who was by now totally mystified.

'I'll make coffee,' Len said. 'You'll have some, Sir Joshua?'

The old man nodded, and Anna went into the kitchen to find cups and saucers. She didn't even know his name.

'Sir Joshua Paul,' Mike said. 'They were squires at Sarvan Hall in the old days, and he's never got out of the habit of taking an interest. Knows everything that goes on, and is fascinated by it. That's why he's lasted so well. This used to be part of the Estate. His old housekeeper retired here and he used to visit often. The old boy's lonely now. No one left.'

George had said the same, and Anna felt a sudden compunction. She could have ridden over again, but she had not wanted to intrude. It had never occurred to her that she might be welcome and that the old man needed contact with people and needed conversation. He was talking now to Dan, who had just come in, and at once slipped into an easy exchange of views on the improvements he had effected.

'Zelie didn't bark at you,' Anna said, suddenly struck by the thought. Zelie barked at everyone who visited.

'She knows my car.' The bitch was sitting with her head against Sir Joshua's knee. 'Old Jenkinson worked for me for a very long time. He was my head gamekeeper. He'd planned to breed Alsatians too, but when his wife died all the stuffing went out of him. I often used to go over and sample their home-made elderberry wine. May Jenkinson was a splendid cook. At one time she cooked for me, and she was always glad of the chance to have me over to supper. I miss them.'

He sighed, regretting the past.

'They knew the old house, and they shared so many memories. One night we went out to catch three poachers. They'd been after the pheasants. One of them was a rough type who turned his gun on me. Jenkinson was creeping up behind them and he grabbed him, and the gun went off and hit a magpie in a nearby tree. Chance in a million. He might have hit me; and then I wouldn't be sitting here. I'm very glad you took my advice. Difficult to remember how you felt that day, eh?'

It was difficult. There was so much to look forward to again. The children would soon be home and Lisa's room was furnished at last, and Susan was now almost part of the family, coming every day with Len. The blind child's mother was beginning to relax.

She was a prickly woman, but maybe that was the result of being a widow with only one child, and that child blind, and no one to talk to until Anna came. She was no longer wary of the dogs. Zelie had converted her, and only last week, watching the endless game that Susan played, following the Alsatian round and round the garden, using the improvised harness that Phil had made, the mother had agreed that a Guide Dog would be a good idea later on.

'Would you like to come to Susan's birthday tea?' Anna asked. She regretted the words as soon as she had spoken them, afraid that Sir Joshua might be offended, but the old face brightened with an impish smile and she suddenly saw a reflection of the boy he had been. A mischievous monkey, she thought.

'He can come if he has his rest,' George said possessively. 'He's not going to overdo it, not even for a birthday party.'

'George is worse than my old nanny,' Sir Joshua said. 'We'll have to go, but not till I've done what I came for. Mike, please will you bring it in.'

Mike grinned at Anna. She watched him walk down the path, a stocky little man with that bushy head of grey-blond hair that flared up from his forehead. He had gentle eyes, and she always loved to watch him when he handled dogs. They all trusted him. Zelie adored him, and the pups always ran to him.

The gate swung to, and opened again.

Mike walked up the path. Beside him paced a regal Alsatian, full grown, a magnificent dog, with a broad wise-eyed head, and a conformation that made Anna's mouth water.

'That is Sarvan Panther. My great-niece bred him. She's very well known in the Alsatian world and this is one of her champions. He's four years old and his sons are already winning. He's mine. But I can't look after him and I'd like to think he lived where he was appreciated and had some home life. He's a

123

gentle, affectionate dog, and he gets miserable in kennels. Mary's got a splendid set-up but it's a very big place and she can't give this fellow individual attention and I can't look after him. I'm much too old and my Sandy would never forgive me if I imported a stranger into the house. He would make a splendid stud for Zelie next time she whelps. You look at his pedigree. You'll find it fits. And he's not carrying any faults that we know of. He's been X-rayed; no hip trouble, and there's never been any sign of it in any of his pups. And no epilepsy. He's been EEG screened to make sure of that. I'd be very grateful if you would take him. I'll make him over to you officially so that there's no trouble with the National Trust; I don't know if they think they own all my property, but I bet they'd try. He's worth a bit.'

'I don't know what to say,' Anna said.

'Then for God's sake don't say anything. Too many women talk too much.' He grinned at her and handed her his coffee cup. 'You'll put my mind at rest. I love that dog, and I mean it. I've watched him grow up and I haven't liked to think of him there by him-self. He's an affectionate beast.'

'Of course I'll take him,' Anna said. 'If you're quite sure . . .'

'Then that's settled. What time's the party?'

Anna watched him walk slowly down the path. 'I hope he doesn't go and die at Susan's party,' Dan said.

'Not him,' said Len. 'He's banking on living to a hundred, and I've never known him fail in anything he's set out to do yet. Barring accidents,' he added.

Anna walked outside. She stroked Panther's head, and he sniffed at her hand. He would have to sleep in the kennels, but so long as neither Zelie nor Amba were in season he could run with them. There might be some rivalry with Argon. They would have to see.

'He's beautiful,' Anna said.

'You made a hit with the old man,' Mike said. 'This fellow is worth well over a thousand pounds. You've got a magnificent stud dog for free.'

'Mike, I can't take him.' Anna stared at him, appalled.

'I suggested it,' Mike said. 'He's been bothered silly over this dog, honest. He's often wondered what to do for the best. His great-niece suggested he found him a good home, as she feels the dog frets without people. He's one of the gentlest Alsatians I know, and I know a good few. There's more nonsense talked about them than about any breed.'

'I thought I said no more dogs,' Dan said softly into her ear, as Mike walked Panther down the garden and put him in the kennel next to Amba.

Anna turned to look at him, but her husband was grinning.

'We can't refuse that one,' he said.

Anna whistled to Zelie and walked over to the pool. There was a glitter of light on the water, and the moorhen chicks were swimming in single file behind their mother. The two geese stood sentinel by the edge of the pool. Beyond them the hedge was green and fresh with spring, and a blackbird sang from a branch of the little willow tree that Dan had planted for her.

Soon it would be time to go in and prepare for the party. She had put a ribbon aside to tie round the neck of the puppy that she was keeping for Susan. One of Zinta's longhairs. And that was another that they would have to keep.

It was no use. They couldn't live without animals. But there would be pups to sell from Zelie and Amba and stud fees from Argon, and surely Panther would earn his keep. Perhaps she could enter him at Cruft's. Perhaps he might even be Best in Breed one year; he was magnificent.

Maybe, too, she would be able to produce an even more splendid dog from him; produce perfect puppies that won prizes all over the world. She looked about her. Setter's Dene had lost its ugliness. It was home, with the garden planted and the pool beyond; with the compound fenced and the kennel block hidden by flowering shrubs that would grow to beauty; with the flowerbeds filled with annuals; and the willow tree growing down by the pool and the ducks and geese swimming.

There were four heads looking at her over the hedge; wise brown eyes and long horse faces. She went to pat Tarquin and Sonny pushed him jealously, and Razzle and Suntan came to butt her arm and ask for pony nuts.

Now there were four horses, they had settled together amicably, pairing off two by two. Wherever Tarquin went, Sonny followed, and the two rescued ponies were inseparable. Phil would love them, and maybe one day they could get Lisa a more spirited horse; and maybe, one day, she could have the brood mare she coveted and breed again. She had loved Syrena and her foals. She needed young stock about the place.

Setter's Dene. To think that she had hated it. Compton Hall would have defeated them in the end; the signs had been there; it was far too big and without labour they had been pushed to their limit. And rising prices were killing all incentive. They never could have survived.

She walked down to the kennel block to make friends with Panther. She let him out and he came to stand beside her, to sniff her all over, identifying every smell; smell of cat and smell of goat and smell of Zelie and a delicious smell of Anna. He leaned against her, tursting her completely. He had never known a real home, or someone of his own to look after him and give him time and give him freedom.

She walked up the garden path with the dog beside her.

Dan was working on the little rockery outside the

living-room window, where she wanted to grow Alpines. He looked up at her.

'Isn't he gorgeous?' she asked. 'Dan, don't you think he could make an all-time champion if I go on and show him? And he'll have fine sons and daughters. He's perfect!'

'You're counting apples again,' Dan said.

Anna laughed and shook her head and held up both hands.

Her fingers were crossed and she held a twig from the willow tree firmly in her fist.

THE END

This book was written for Belinda Pilling
in memory of
Velindre Gorsefield Poirot (Porky)
my Alsatian's litter brother,
who died of lead poisoning at 7 months old.

JOYCE STRANGER NOVELS AVAILABLE IN CORGI PAPERBACKS

WHILE EVERY EFFORT IS MADE TO KEEP PRICES LOW, IT IS SOME-TIMES NECESSARY TO INCREASE PRICES AT SHORT NOTICE. CORGI BOOKS RESERVE THE RIGHT TO SHOW NEW RETAIL PRICES ON COVERS WHICH MAY DIFFER FROM THOSE PREVIOUSLY ADVERTISED IN THE TEXT OR ELSEWHERE.

THE PRICES SHOWN BELOW WERE CORRECT AT THE TIME OF GOING TO PRESS (FEBRUARY '83).

☐	12044 8	THE MONASTERY CAT AND OTHER ANIMALS	£1.50
☐	11951 2	THREE'S A PACK	£1.50
☐	09893 0	BREED OF GIANTS	85p
☐	11803 6	HOW TO OWN A SENSIBLE DOG (NF)	£1.25
☐	08141 8	REX	£1.25
☐	08394 1	CASEY	£1.25
☐	08633 9	RUSTY	£1.25
☐	08931 1	ZARA	£1.25
☐	10685 2	FLASH	£1.25
☐	10695 X	KYM	£1.25

All these books are available at your book shop or newsagent, or can be ordered direct from the publisher. Just tick the titles you want and fill in the form below.

CORGI BOOKS, Cash Sales Department, P.O. Box 11, Falmouth, Cornwall.

Please send cheque or postal order, no currency.

Please allow cost of book(s) plus the following for postage and packing:

U.K. Customers—Allow 45p for the first book, 20p for the second book and 14p for each additional book ordered, to a maximum charge of £1.63.

B.F.P.O. and Eire—Allow 45p for the first book, 20p for the second book plus 14p per copy for the next 7 books, thereafter 8p per book.

Overseas Customers—Allow 75p for the first book and 21p per copy for each additional book.

NAME (Block Letters) ....

ADDRESS ....

....